MW01137559

Books By Keely Brooke Keith

Uncharted

Uncharted Beginnings

Uncharted Journey

KEELY BROOKE KEITH

Edenbrooke
Press

*"Good people take care of their animals,
but wicked people are cruel to theirs."*
–Proverbs 12:10 (GNT)

CHAPTER ONE

Half of Eva Vestal's heart was buried in the shade of an old gray leaf tree on the east side of the Inn at Falls Creek; the other half was strong enough to pull a plow, but as long as she managed the inn well, she wouldn't have to.

Eva controlled her footing as she tiptoed between the toy marbles scattered in the office doorway. She sidestepped her six-year-old son, who was sitting on the rag rug, picking out the red marbles to work the addition equations on his slate. Zeke's chalk screeched against the board, making the only sound in the otherwise quiet inn.

Eva shifted the two heavy inventory books she was holding to the other arm and glanced at Zeke's slate. Once again, all of his answers were correct. "Good job, sweetie."

Zeke looked up at her with deep-set eyes, just like his father's. "Write some more, please, Mama." A short whistle followed his every *S* sound, thanks to a missing front tooth.

"You are getting good at arithmetic. I'm proud of you." Eva slid the thick inventory ledgers onto her desk and wiped Zeke's slate with her apron. "Want to try something a little harder? Maybe adding double digits?"

Zeke wrinkled his freckled nose. "What are double digits?"

"Numbers higher than nine but lower than one hundred."

He looked at her like she'd ask him to hitch up the wagon and drive it clear to Good Springs. "Mama, I'm only six!"

A light chuckle vibrated Eva's throat. "All right, we can save double digits for another day." She gripped the dusty piece of chalk and wrote more equations on his slate. "But I will give you some eights and nines." She probably should have started his schooling last year, but she always had more work than daylight and would until Revel moved back home. Her fingertips tapped the ledger books. "You will have to learn to add big numbers to help run the inn someday."

Zeke took his slate and plopped back down on the rug between the office doorway and Eva's desk. He frowned. "I don't want to run the inn when I grow up. That's a lady job."

"No, it isn't. Your grandpa ran the inn before he married your grandma, and your great-grandfather ran the inn *and* the stables *and* farmed. And your Uncle Revel will run the inn when he inherits it someday."

Probably someday soon, but she kept that part to herself.

Zeke corralled his marbles between his knobby ankles. His trousers were too short for his growing legs, but Eva didn't have time to make him a new pair this week. Maybe Claudia could do it. He picked up two red marbles and held them over his face, pretending they were his eyeballs. "I don't want a job that keeps me inside the house all day."

He'd gotten that from his father too. Funny what a kid could inherit from a parent he had never met.

Zeke shuffled his marbles on the rug, and a few rolled to the hardwood floor and into the hallway. He crawled after them. "When I'm grown up, I'll work in the stables and have a big white horse and name him Jack."

Eva smiled at her son, glad he was looking forward to a life at the inn. He would have to work in the stables and do a lot more around here if Revel didn't move back.

As Zeke wiggled his legs, more marbles rolled into the corridor. Eva used her pencil to point at the wayward glass globes. "Pick all those up. If your grandpa or Leonard walks past, they might slip. When older folks fall down, they don't pop back up like kids do."

"Yes, Mama." He'd inherited his compliant nature from his father too.

Eva sat at her desk and flipped the reservation book open to today: *Wednesday, March 21, 2029*. The first day of autumn in the Land. The end of summer had come to the southern hemisphere too quickly this year. If winter brought winds as frigid as last year's, her father and Leonard might both be crippled by their arthritis. There was no way either of them could work out-of-doors another winter. She had to either convince Revel to come home now or find the right men to take over the jobs.

She glanced out the window opposite her desk. The mid-morning sun cast the big gray leaf tree's shadow over the grass between the inn and the greenhouse. Beneath the high limbs of the old tree, an iron bench sat near three engraved stone markers. Her grandfather and grandmother's graves were close together and her husband was buried a few feet away from them. She'd spent three months as his wife then almost seven years as his widow and God had carried her through every heartbroken day.

A stone bridge arched over Falls Creek just beyond the gray leaf tree. None of the other buildings on the inn's property were visible from the office windows. Her father always said it shouldn't matter to her because her job was to welcome incoming travelers, not worry about the stables or the farm.

As the inn's manager it all mattered to her. If it weren't for her efforts to get temporary workers, this place wouldn't be able to sustain itself and stay open for the travelers on the lonely road across the Land.

She traced a finger down today's reservation listing. The Overseer of Clover Ridge and his wife should arrive today. Their letter had requested a three-night stay, depending on how their journey was going thus far. She would give them Room 5. That would leave one more double room open in case a family came through later. The three other guest rooms upstairs were already occupied.

Two traders from Northcrest were staying again tonight in the bunkhouse, so she had four remaining beds available out there. Solomon Cotter, the horse breeder from Riverside, was scheduled to return this week since both the mares he'd bred his stallion with were due to foal soon. It seemed like a waste of time to come all the way out here just for the birth of two horses, but Solo had insisted and Eva's father had been quick to agree with him. Solo could stay in the bunkhouse like he usually did.

So that left her with one double room upstairs and three empty beds in the bunkhouse. "Plenty of space tonight," she said aloud, even though Zeke wasn't listening.

His marbles clinked as he added them.

She looked out at the empty road. "Maybe someone will show up who needs permanent work and just happens to know how to run the stables or the farm. We need a man for each job. Someone with references and experience and the desire to stay out here for good." And someone so impressive her father actually allowed her to make the hire.

She opened one of the inventory books. The bottom of the first column listed only twelve tins of lantern fuel. "Let's also hope a trader from Woodland comes through this week."

"Hm?" Zeke asked.

"Nothing, sweetie."

The side screen door creaked open and slapped against the inn's clapboard exterior, echoing through the hallway. Her father's gravelly voice followed the racket. "Sorry, very sorry. Wind caught the door again." Frederick Roberts hobbled into the office's doorway and leaned against the jamb. He hadn't set foot inside the office since he'd made Eva the inn's manager five years ago. He sniffed the air. "What's Sybil cooking?"

A hint of browning meat and onions teased Eva's nose. "Smells like she is starting a roast for this evening."

Little Zeke held up his slate. "Look, Grandpa, I can add nines!"

"Good boy. Very good boy, indeed." Frederick scratched his chin through his long white whiskers and gazed at Eva. Though it was only ten in the morning, his bloodshot eyes looked like he'd been awake for days. "There was something I meant to tell you, Peach."

"What is it?" Eva asked as she turned the page in the inventory book to check the farm supply figures. The hardware list hadn't been updated in months. She would see to it after lunch, unless Claudia needed help with the housekeeping chores.

She looked up at her father, who hadn't answered her yet. He was staring out the window toward the front yard. She followed her father's line of sight. The inn's shadow darkened the south lawn. The equinox would begin Earth's tilt away from the sun. Soon the Antarctic winds would creep across the hills, whistle through the window shutters, and frost the panes.

But it wasn't the weather that was on her father's mind when he stared out at the road like that. It was Mother.

Zeke handed Eva his slate, breaking her thoughts. "Mama, can I go outside with Leonard now?"

"It's *may I go*. And yes, you may. Be careful!"

He tore out of the room like any young boy freed from schoolwork.

Eva held up his slate to show her father Zeke's work. "It's a good thing he is a quick learner because he won't sit still for long lessons."

Frederick jolted from his reverie when the screen door slammed. "That boy is just like Revel."

"No, he isn't." The betrayal of Revel leaving her to manage the inn made any comparison of her son to her brother unacceptable. "Little Zeke is just like his father. Ezekiel never would have abandoned his responsibilities."

Her father gave her a look and patted the air. "Calm down, Peach. I meant Zeke reminds me of Revel when he was that age. He just wanted to get gone."

"Wanting to be out-of-doors is not the same as…" Eva stood, hoping it would urge her father to forget about his prodigal son and remember his business so she could work on the inventory lists. "What did you want to tell me, Father?"

He pressed his lips together. "Can't remember now."

"It will come to you." She picked up the ledger. "I have to go over the pantry list with Sybil before she gets too busy."

Frederick didn't budge from the doorway. He hooked a thumb in his suspenders and mumbled, "I think it had something to do with the horses."

"Let me know when you remember."

"Or a guest room…"

"Maybe if you walk out to the stable block and back it will jog your memory."

He shifted his weight and grimaced. "My knees can't take any extra walking today."

She lowered her volume even though no guests were in the house at the moment. "Please, look over the reference letters for the man from Southpoint. I think he would manage the farm just fine and so does his former employer. Then, you and Leonard could split the stable work until we find a second man."

Frederick snapped his face toward her, the green of his eyes glowing resolutely. "This is still my inn, Peach, and I say who we hire and when. As long as I have a son out there," he jabbed a crooked finger at the window, "who will inherit all this, I'm waiting for him to come home."

Though he was her father, some days it was more like talking to a child than a parent. Eva took a slow breath to keep her emotions from entering her voice. "Even if

Revel returns to the inn soon, you still need to hire one more man. Leonard's back aches as much as your knees do. He requires more and more help with the farming every month. We can't keep asking more traders to stay extra days to do all the work. We need to hire a permanent man to take over for Leonard."

Frederick rapidly shook his head. "Whoever we hire will work alongside Revel his whole life, just like Leonard has worked with me. That's why Revel should have a say in this."

Eva hugged the inventory book to her chest. Revel might never come back, but she didn't have the heart to tell her father that anymore. His son had left. His wife had left. Her husband had died. No one needed reminding, but he did need to face the truth just like she'd had to long ago. "Father, I want Revel to return as much as you do. But for now, we need to hire two men so we can keep this place running."

CHAPTER TWO

Solomon Cotter clicked at his Shire stallion, encouraging the brawny horse to pull the wagon up another hill. "Almost there, King. Keep going, boy!"

The draft horse snorted as if this steep hill were nothing to him, just like the hill before it.

Solo chuckled. "Maybe it isn't difficult for you, but most horses tucker out climbing away from the river valley."

The dirt road's wheel tracks disappeared over the hill ahead. Golden-topped grasses waved along the side of the road. The open country out here in the middle of the Land was the kind of place a man could be himself, free of routine and ridicule and tyrannical ranch bosses who made their employees miserable.

The wagon bumped and rattled on the rocky road despite King's smooth pull, but the three-month-old puppy relaxing against Solo's leg didn't care. The little dog was fast asleep as if the wagon bench were a comfy bed.

King's muscles contracted under his shiny black coat while he pulled the wagon steadily up the hill. Once atop it, he lifted his regal head toward the inn, wordlessly proclaiming their imminent arrival.

Solo cast his gaze across the sweeping landscape and whistled one long note. The sharp noise woke the puppy. It looked up at Solo with its eyes half shut.

Solo stroked the fuzzy fur between the dog's ears. "It's beautiful country out here, isn't it?"

Tree-dotted hills rolled in shades of greens and browns to the western horizon, which was broken in the distance by the stately Inn at Falls Creek. The two-story home's white clapboard siding shone majestically in the afternoon sunlight, setting it apart from the azure sky and drying grass. Flanked by an L-shaped stable block, the inn stood like a proud general in front of an army of outbuildings, a cottage, and a bunkhouse.

Solo had slept in that bunkhouse more nights than he could count. However, he knew the number of nights' stay he had saved up. According to Frederick Roberts' last letter, Solo had accumulated forty nights' accommodation through extra trade and the successful breeding of King to two of the inn's mares. Frederick had agreed to Solo's request to redeem those forty nights consecutively. And Frederick had said he would keep the reason for that long of a stay private.

That was one of the best parts about the inn— Frederick's fairness and understanding. Sybil's cooking was a close second. The Roberts family's generous hospitality made running the Land's only inn look easy. Romantic almost. Even Frederick's little grandson, Zeke, was already learning the business.

And Solo was about to make good on a promise to the boy. He took his eyes off the road long enough to glance at the young herding dog lying beside him. "Pup, I have a feeling you're going to like your new owner."

King pulled the wagon over the stone bridge that crossed Falls Creek, and Solo's teeth clattered from the jiggling. Sunlight glinted between the branches of a mature gray leaf tree as Solo drove past. The family had added an iron bench beneath the old tree since his last visit. Must be a nice place to relax in the shade.

A pair of gossiping chickens fluttered off the drive and out of King's way as he pulled the wagon past the inn and toward the stable block. Solo parked the wagon in front of the stable's arched opening then jumped down and stretched his stiff legs. The puppy stood on the bench, wagging its white and brown tail.

Solo tied King's lines to the brake and gave the horse a quick pat. "Good job, boy. I'll get you unhitched and to the trough in no time."

"Come on, pup." He cradled the wiggly dog in the crook of his arm.

Frederick Roberts limped toward Solo from the house. The older man's gait was a little slower and a lot more labored than the last time Solo had seen him. Frederick squinted as he approached the wagon and he called out, "That you, Solo?"

Solo stepped around the wagon to meet the inn's owner. "Yes, sir. It's me." He shifted the puppy to his left side and stuck out his right hand. "It's good to see you."

Frederick's handshake hadn't lost any strength. "Welcome back, son. Still planning on a long stay this time?"

"If that's still all right with you."

"It's fine. Just fine." He pointed over his shoulder at the inn. "I'll let Eva know about our arrangement."

"I thought your daughter knew I was coming."

"Well, she expected your arrival for the foals' births, but I forgot to tell her how long you plan to stay."

Solo was eager to settle in somewhere quiet and start writing. The last thing he needed was a take-charge woman taking charge of his stories. Or worse yet, criticizing him for wanting to write a children's storybook. He looked at Frederick. "Can we still keep my plans between us… at least until I get into a good stride with my writing? I already have a dozen of the stories outlined, but it will take some concentrating to get them all down on paper in forty days."

Frederick gave Solo's back a vigorous pat. "I'll do my best to protect your privacy, but Eva catches wind of everything around here. Your endeavor won't go unnoticed for long."

A young voice shouted in the distance, "Mr. Cotter! Mr. Cotter!" Zeke ran toward him from the barn at full speed, dust swirling in the young boy's wake. He didn't stop until he was toe-to-toe with Solo. "Is that your puppy?"

"No." Solo glanced at Frederick, who was smiling at his grandson. He held the dog out to Zeke. "This is your puppy. We had a deal, remember?"

"Mine?" Zeke's eyes sparkled as he took the little dog in his arms. His tight hold made it squirm. "What deal?"

"Last time I was here, I told you if you were good for your mama, I would bring you a puppy from the ranch where I work in Riverside." He pointed at Frederick. "Your grandfather told me in his letter that you have been well-behaved and you help your mama out. Is that still true?"

"Oh yes, sir!" Zeke giggled while the puppy licked his face. "Can I keep her?"

"It's a boy and he's all yours. What are you going to name him?"

Zeke gave the dog a hug then set it on the ground, rubbing its fur all the while. "I'll name him Joshua."

Solo smiled at Zeke's quick reply. "Why Joshua?"

"Grandpa told us about Joshua when we had our church time on Sunday. I like the name."

"Fair enough." Solo tousled the boy's hair then stood. "I know you will take good care of him."

"Yes, sir!" Zeke's bowl-cut brown hair bounced as he ran to the grassy yard with the puppy yapping at his heels. "Thank you, Mr. Cotter!"

"You're welcome." Solo turned to Frederick, who was watching his grandson play with the dog. "I hope his mother doesn't mind."

"You're about to find out." The older man motioned toward the inn. "Here she comes now."

Over the years that Solo had been stopping at the inn during his travels for the ranch, the only thing that had changed about Eva was her last name from Roberts to Vestal. She marched toward them wearing the warm smile of a kind neighbor and the determined gaze of a shrewd businesswoman. Loose strands of dark hair blew off her shoulder as if getting out of her way while the getting was good. She may not have changed outwardly, but her fierceness had grown. When she reached the wagon, King shuffled a few inches to the side.

Solo gave his horse a calming pat then offered the inn's manager a smile. "Afternoon, Eva."

"Good afternoon, Solo. How was your journey?"

The breeze carried the scents of soap and spice from her skin, briefly distracting him from her question. "It was… peaceful."

"I'm pleased to hear it." She lifted her pixie-like chin at the grass beside the barn where Zeke was running with his new dog. "Is that a puppy he's playing with?"

"Yes, ma'am. I gave it to him."

She stared at her son and the dog for a moment, her symmetrically arched brows slightly raised.

Solo's stomach turned. He should have gotten her permission before giving a dog to her son. At the time, telling Frederick in his correspondence seemed like enough, but now standing near Eva, he wasn't so sure. The woman emitted an authority powerful enough to knock over a mule.

Solo opened his mouth to explain himself but stopped when thin lines curved around Eva's mouth. A grin broke through her imperial expression. "That was very thoughtful of you. Zeke could use a friend out here."

Solo almost sighed in relief.

Eva snapped her attention to the contents of his wagon. "You brought more than usual. Is this all for trade?"

"Some of it. The trunk is mine though."

She gave one brisk nod. "Do you need help to carry it to the bunkhouse?"

Frederick lumbered between them. "Solo will stay in a guest room upstairs during his visit this time."

The creamy skin of Eva's forehead furrowed. "I don't have any single rooms available tonight."

Frederick shook his head. "He will stay in Room Four."

"A double? No offense, Solomon." She glanced at him then at her father. "A single man doesn't need a double."

Frederick ignored her and looked at Solo. "The double room on the northeast corner of the inn has the extra space you will need. It should suit you just fine for… how long was it we said?"

"Forty days."

"That's right."

The outer corner of Eva's left eye twitched. Her voice took on a sharpness that could cut glass. "Forty days?"

Solo wanted away from her before she erupted. He kept his focus on Frederick. "It will suit me fine, sir. Thank you."

"Father!" Eva crossed her lean arms. "Why so long?"

"He has saved up the payment for a forty-night stay in trade with me."

"But a single man doesn't need a double room. Do you, Solomon?" She spit her question with such force he nearly agreed just to stay on her good side.

Frederick lifted a hand, halting his daughter's protest. "Solo and I have an arrangement, Peach." He motioned to the back of the wagon. "Take your trunk upstairs, son. Eva will get you the key to Room Four." Then he turned to the paddock and rubbed his abdomen. "Where in blazes did it go?"

Eva uncrossed her arms and concern changed her expression. "Where did what go, Father?"

"The outhouse." Frederick pointed vaguely at the pasture. "It used to be right over there. Who moved it? Where did it go? I can't go back into the house with dirty boots or Mother will yell at me."

Eva moved close to her father's side and whispered. "You can go into the house. It's all right." She flashed a worried glance at Solo then gently took Frederick's arm. "Come on, Father. I'll take you inside."

CHAPTER THREE

The inviting aroma of slow-roasted venison filled the inn as Eva carried dinner plates into the bustling dining hall. She slid the full plates onto the table in front of the guests. Steam rose from the buttery mashed potatoes, and pan gravy ran around the hunks of tender meat and garlicky green beans. Her sister's cooking made her mouth water.

Zeke sat next to Frederick and across from Leonard and Claudia at the family's table in the corner of the room. Her son's hungry gaze seared the meat on their plates better than any skillet would have. "Mama," he whined impatiently.

The sooner he learned that guests come first the better. She held up a finger to him. "I'll be right back with yours and Grandpa's."

Leonard snapped open his napkin and tucked it into his collar. His back hunched, making his chin protrude over his plate. Claudia folded her hands, waiting for everyone to have food before she picked up her fork. Leonard took Claudia's hand and gazed at her sweetly, his weathered fingers caressing her swollen knuckles.

They had spent fifty years working at the inn—Leonard as the inn's farmer and Claudia as the housekeeper. Now approaching their seventies, they seemed more in love with each other every year.

That was the life Eva was supposed to have with her late husband. The shock of losing him had faded in the seven years since his death, its edges dulled and less likely to slice her heart open, but the old ache never left. Claudia always said it was because grief was fueled by love, and since she'd loved Ezekiel with all her heart, her whole heart was scarred by his death.

Frederick put his arm over the back of Zeke's chair. "Your mama serves us last, but we get the biggest portions." He winked at Eva. "Isn't that right, Peach?"

It wasn't right. It was an odd thing for her father to say, but such comments were coming from him more often of late. Eva tried to ignore the dread building in her chest. She put on her public smile. "Sure, so long as you wash dishes to pay for your keep."

A few of the men at the next table laughed. Solomon Cotter forked potatoes into his mouth and gave Eva a closed-lip grin as she passed his table. He wiggled his eyebrows as if trying to get an extra smile out of her. He'd already gotten a double room and a long-term stay. He wasn't getting special attention too.

She took a quick second look at the scar that divided Solo's left eyebrow vertically, then dashed into the kitchen to get more plates from the countertop. Sybil Roberts was ladling gravy on a hefty portion of meat. "This should make sixteen plates. Is that all, Eva?"

"Don't forget yours and mine."

Her sister nodded and took two more pewter plates off the shelf above the countertop. She blew a stray brown curl off her forehead as she fished chunks of roast out of the stove pot. "Full house?"

"I'll say. Two of the single rooms will have men sleeping on cots tonight."

Sybil frowned. "I always feel sorry for the men who sleep on cots."

"Most of them don't mind. They have been on the road, sleeping on the ground or in the back of a wagon for so long that they are just happy to be indoors." She picked up the last two plates. "Everyone is complimenting your roast. After I serve Zeke and Father, I'll come sit in here with you."

When Eva walked back into the dining hall, her little Zeke was telling everyone at his table and the table next to him about his new puppy. He had half the room's attention. "And he likes to chew sticks and I named him Joshua and I'm going to make him a red collar." He looked at Claudia. "Do you have any red fabric I can use for his collar?"

The older woman stopped with her fork halfway to her mouth and grinned at Zeke. "I'm sure I can scrounge up something."

Zeke continued talking about his new puppy. "He's a fast runner and I'm teaching him to shake hands. Mr. Cotter gave him to me," he announced, pointing at Solo.

A trader from Good Springs who was sitting next to Solo gave him a thump on the shoulder. Both men watched Eva as she passed the table again to leave the room. If she acknowledged them, they would want to talk to her. Her stomach rumbled, begging for dinner. She hurried out of the dining room, through the short hallway, and into the kitchen.

Sybil had both of their plates waiting on the kitchen's dinette table. She was sitting in her usual seat where she could see the door should anyone come from the dining hall needing anything.

Eva sat across from her sister and filled her water cup. "Did you hear what Father did?"

Sybil shook her head, too polite to speak with her mouth full.

"He gave Room Four to Solomon Cotter. A double. Father didn't even ask me first. Didn't even look at the reservation book. Thank the Lord no families arrived today." She paused long enough to take a bite of roast. The delicious meat's savory flavor briefly made her forget her troubles. As soon as she swallowed, she remembered them again. "And not just for the night. No, no. Father told him he could stay here for forty nights."

She watched her younger sister, waiting for her to appear surprised.

Sybil simply nodded as she listened and ate, so Eva tried again. "Forty nights! Isn't that ridiculous? Neither of them would tell me why so long. Father said Solo had saved up the nights and they had a deal. He shut me right up. I am the inn's manager. Why did Father give me the office and title and responsibilities if he wasn't going to give me the authority to make decisions?"

Eva stabbed her fork into the meat a little harder than intended and it screeched on the plate. Her mother would have slapped her hand for that. She flashed a mock grimace to Sybil, and her sister giggled like she did when they were children. But Sybil still hadn't reacted to their father's arrangement with Solo, so Eva asked, "Does it seem like Father is behaving oddly to you lately?"

Sybil dabbed her mouth with her napkin. "He's just getting forgetful. In mother's last letter, she said Grandma and Grandpa are that way too but much worse. That's why she can't come to visit us. She has to stay with them every moment. She says Grandpa wanders off if she doesn't keep an eye on him."

There was more to their mother's decision to go live with her parents in Southpoint eight years ago than their health, but no one acknowledged it. Eva pinched off a corner of her bread roll and popped it into her mouth. "I wonder if that's what is happening to Father. He's so much older than Mother—almost the same age as Grandpa and Grandma. Lately, he can't remember what he intended to do when he walks from one room to the next. Seems to me like Solo is taking advantage of Father's forgetfulness."

Sybil shook her head. "Mr. Cotter isn't like that."

"Maybe you're right. But, Father is getting too old to—"

"Excuse me," a man's voice said from the doorway. Eva looked over her shoulder to see the trader from Good Springs.

Sybil stood and dropped her napkin on her chair. "What can I get for you?"

"Nothing, ma'am." He motioned for her to sit back down. "The food is quite good. Can't remember when I last had such a meal." He slid his hand into his breast pocket and withdrew a creased envelope. "I have a letter for Eva." He held the envelope out and inched into the kitchen as if it were forbidden territory.

Eva met him mid-way. "Thank you."

"Sorry, I forgot to give it to you earlier. I felt it in my pocket just now and remembered." He backed out of the room.

"Thank you all the same." Eva sat and opened the envelope made of gray leaf paper. The letter was folded over several times, but she immediately recognized the sloppy pencil writing. "It's from Revel."

Sybil froze with her water cup at her lips. "What does it say?"

Eva read slowly, trying to decipher his scribbles. "He will be staying with the Colburns in Good Springs for a while longer. He is working with the outsider, Connor Bradshaw, on organizing the Land's security force."

Sybil lifted her thin brows. "Sounds exciting."

"It does, doesn't it?" She lowered the letter. "He probably will never come back."

"Did he say that?"

"No." She blew out a long breath. "When Revel was a kid, all he ever wanted to do was go with the traders all around the Land. As soon as he turned eighteen, he did just that. He's been living as he pleases for a decade now. I doubt he will settle down just because Father's arthritis is acting up."

Sybil lowered her volume even though the chatter in the dining hall was so loud no one in the other room could have heard them. "Maybe if you wrote to Revel about Father's forgetfulness and just how badly his knees pain him… maybe then he would know you are serious."

"I did."

Her sister raised a palm. "And?"

She held out the letter to Sybil. "Here. Read it yourself."

Sybil didn't take the paper. "What will you do?"

"I don't know." Eva leaned her tired back into the chair. "We need two more permanent workers—one for Father's job and one for Leonard's. Father doesn't approve of anyone I suggest and says it's not up to me to hire more men, but I must do something."

"Will you hire someone without his approval?"

"How can I?" She refolded Revel's letter, not wanting to see his handwriting for another minute. "If I did and Father told them to leave, they would obey him and not me. Besides, it's not easy to find men willing to move away from the villages. And I would need to find married men, or at least one of them should be married so his wife can take on some of Claudia's work. She won't be able to manage the laundry and cleaning the rooms forever."

Sybil set down her fork. "I know. I had to help in the laundry house this morning. Of course…" She grinned a little and got a mischievous look as if hatching a secret plan.

"Of course what?"

"Well, if you hired single men, maybe…"

"Maybe what?"

"Maybe you could have a…"

"A what?"

"A companion. And Zeke could have a daddy."

If an adorable smile hadn't immediately followed Sybil's remark, Eva would have become defensive. "Very funny, Syb."

Her sister looked up at the ceiling. "Perhaps it's time?"

"I beg your pardon." Eva couldn't entertain the idea of marrying again—wouldn't let herself even imagine it—or she would get sick with guilt at the thought of betraying her late husband. "Zeke has his grandpa and

Leonard for father figures. I think he is doing just fine without a daddy."

Sybil leaned forward. "What about you?"

"I already have one father to deal with and that's plenty, thank you."

"No." Sybil chuckled. "I meant what about you getting married again? You know, someday?"

"I know what you meant, and no."

"Ever?"

Eva stuffed Revel's letter into her apron pocket and stood, her stomach uncomfortably full. She picked up her empty plate and Sybil's to take them to the sink. "Never ever."

CHAPTER FOUR

Bailey Colburn gripped the yacht's rusted railing as the sun sank below the horizon, taking with it all hope of finding the Land. For two weeks she'd spent every heartbeat trying to reach these exact coordinates on this exact day. All that work and worry for nothing. Maybe she would get another chance next year.

Yeah, right.

Bailey's iron stomach stayed steady as the repurposed charter yacht bobbed up and down in the choppy waters of the South Atlantic Ocean. The wind whipped her cropped hair into her vision as she glanced over her shoulder at the windows behind her. Four men's silhouettes moved inside the yacht's bridge.

Professor Timothy Van Buskirk stepped close to the window. His fatherly eyes gazed out at Bailey from beneath the brim of his white bucket hat—his *lucky hat* he called it. He motioned for her to join him in the bridge. The corners of his gray mustache flattened in disappointment. She was grateful to Professor Tim for convincing his nephew, Micah, to bring them out here on one of his company's yachts, but she had let them down.

Never again would Micah Van Buskirk agree to sail to the middle of nowhere hoping to see a peaceful and pristine land suddenly appear like Atlantis rising out of the mist. Maybe if the world were like it was before the war, Micah would brush off this massive failure and raise his glass to searching for the Land again next year. But nothing was like it was before the war.

Over the past several years, desperate nations had sent more bombs flying than a 2020 action movie. Between the battles, the water poisonings, and the plague, only a fraction of earth's pre-war population was left. The fact that Bailey and her former professor made it to the middle of the South Atlantic to chase a fantasy was a miracle. And a waste.

Wasted resources, wasted connections, wasted time. Micah would probably give Bailey an earful at dinner tonight. He hadn't wanted to take time away from his humanitarian work of using the yacht to run medical supplies to remote islands in the South Atlantic, but he'd obliged his uncle's request.

At least, Professor Tim wouldn't be upset with Bailey. He never was.

No matter how the guys reacted tonight, this trip had been worth the shot. Trying to find the Land had let Bailey imagine a life worth living—a life of plentiful food, unpolluted water, simple pleasures, and maybe even connecting with her long-lost relatives.

When she'd told Professor Tim about the Land's existence, it had given him hope for his future too. And no matter how inconvenienced Micah acted by their request, he'd also been intrigued by the notion of a hidden land untouched by the third world war.

Now, she'd disappointed all of them. She never should have believed a word Justin Mercer said, especially about his time spent in a hidden land settled in the 1860s by a group of peaceful American families—one of which she was supposedly related to. Justin said Bailey had family somewhere and that was all it took to get her to work for him.

Turned out, Justin Mercer was a liar.

The last ray of sunlight slipped below the watery horizon, abruptly ending the day. Diamond-bright stars punctured the clear black sky. And just like that, the day was gone along with her dream of a safe and simple life with the cousins she'd never known.

As Bailey walked toward the ship's bridge, Micah and his two South African crewmen stepped out to the deck. Both of the sun-bleached crewmen wore high-caliber handguns holstered to their sides. Bailey kept her gaze forward as she entered the bridge but watched the crewmen with her peripheral vision.

Inside the bridge Professor Tim stood near the helm, holding his eyeglasses in one hand and rubbing the length of his nose with the other. He put his glasses back on and looked at Bailey in the same way he did the day he told her all Eastern Shore University classes were canceled until the war was over. And like that day, he'd waited until the room was empty so he could speak to her privately—a kindness often extended to the less fortunate.

Well, she wasn't a downtrodden foster kid anymore and hadn't been for eight years. She could handle bad news. She could also take care of herself. She didn't need pity, even from the only person left who cared about her.

She pushed the shaggy ends of her sable hair out of her eyes and marched forward, speaking before Professor Tim had the chance. "Look, I know this is the correct location. I saw the Land on the satellite image on Justin Mercer's computer. And he had evidence—the gray leaf tree saplings. You said yourself the saplings were unlike anything on the planet. You know the Land is out here." Tim raised a halting hand, but she ignored it. "We just need to give it one more day. The Land will appear. I know it will."

"How do you know?"

"I can feel it."

"You're a scientist." Tim lowered his chin to look at her over the rim of his glasses. "If you can't see it or measure it or detect it, forget it."

"This is different. We're exploring the unknown. The satellite image Justin showed me, the gray leaf tree, everything about the Land... it's different from lab experiments." She looked past Tim and out the bridge windows. Micah and the crewmen were working on the lighted deck. Everything beyond the yacht's railing was black, but the ocean and sky were out there, and somewhere not too far away, was a hidden land.

Or so she hoped.

Reality's despair wrestled with her heart's desire. "The Land's existence goes against our modern knowledge and believing Justin Mercer went against my better judgment, but the gray leaf tree saplings changed everything for me. The gray leaf is unclassifiable, miraculous if what Justin said about its medicinal property is true. I can't give up on finding the Land. Not yet."

Tim tapped one of the computer screens embedded in the yacht's instrument panel. Navigational readings appeared on the screen. "Even if it's true and the Land is out there, the exact moment of the equinox has passed. The Land won't be accessible again for another year, according to Mr. Mercer." He looked up at her with kind but tired eyes. "We gave it our best shot. Micah knows these waters. He says we are in more danger of being pirated every hour we drift out here."

"Yes, and he also said the instruments were going berserk this afternoon."

"We must sail back to Tristan de Cunah before we run into trouble. I don't want you kids getting hurt."

Bailey jabbed a thumb toward the window as the two crewmen walked across the yacht's deck. "We will be fine as long as we have Armed and Dangerous with us." She smiled playfully.

The draw cord hanging from Tim's lucky hat swung beneath his chin as he shook his head. Their inside jokes about the trigger-happy crewmen were over, as was their adventure. "Look Bailey, I'm sorry this didn't work out. I wanted this for you as much—more maybe—than you wanted it for yourself. You deserve a better life… and to meet your relatives." He tilted his head. "But hey, can't a person make a family out of friends?"

She nodded, acknowledging the end of their effort more than his question. "Thanks for trying."

He grinned slightly. "Thank you for trusting me with the secret of the Land."

"Seriously?"

"Yes, seriously. This was the most fun I've had in years." His grin faded. "The only fun I've had in years. It was worth it."

The bridge door opened. As Micah stepped inside, a blast of thunder cracked the sky above him, shaking the boat. The jolt threw him to the floor. Lightning burst across the clear night sky in every direction. The two crewmen hurried below deck, cursing the sudden electrical storm.

As bolts of virescent light ignited the sky, an eerie hum vibrated the yacht. The ship's power went out, and the skin along Bailey's neck prickled. The tight space in the bridge shrank even more in the dark. Suddenly, she felt like her five-year-old self locked in the closet again. Her fists lifted instinctively as if she were about to spar an unseen opponent. After a few seconds of darkness, a caged backup light flickered to life on the wall above the door, but she still wanted out of the shrinking space.

Bailey lowered her guarding hands. "What's going on?"

Professor Tim knelt beside his nephew, whose face was wrenched in agony. "Micah! Are you all right?"

Micah sucked in air through clenched teeth. "My arm. I think it's broken."

The bridge door swung on its hinge as the boat pitched. The low hum intensified, rattling the floorboards. Bailey lunged for the door and closed it, but it didn't muffle the sound. Her fingertips tingled as she touched the metal knob. Outside the windows specks of light popped in the air like fireflies spontaneously combusting. "Tim! You have to see this!"

Tim sent her a concerned scowl from under the brim of his white hat. "Get away from the windows!"

Thunder rumbled and a deafening snap resounded from deep within the ship. The bridge shook, buckling

Bailey's legs, but she didn't lose her balance. "What's happening?"

Micah groaned as he forced himself to his knees, holding his crooked right arm against his body. Tim tried to stop him, but Micah crawled toward the instrument panel. "The lightning knocked out our electrical system."

Bailey braced a hand against the wall when one of the crewmen opened the door. He cursed as the lightning flashed again. "We're taking on water down below!" Then he said to Micah, "We need to board the tenders!"

Micah shook his head, his words stunted by pain. "It's not safe out there."

As quickly as it had started, the lightning stopped. The ship's floor stilled. Bailey scanned the darkness outside the windows. The specks of light flickering in the air dissolved.

A brief wave of relief passed through the room, but before anyone spoke, the ship listed portside. The second crewman staggered into the doorway. "It'd be safer out there in a tender than it's about to be in here. The hull is cracked."

While the four men argued about whether they should abandon the ship, something outside the windows caught Bailey's attention. A full moon crested the earth directly ahead, and silhouettes of trees broke the horizon. "Land!" Bailey yelled, silencing the men. "Look, there is land! It has to be *the* Land!"

She rushed out the bridge door, her excited heart pounding in her chest like it had when she won her first martial arts tournament. But something was odd. The moon appeared oval rather than round as though it had been stretched out. Before she could focus on it, a distinct and familiar scent filled the air. She inhaled deeply then looked back at Professor Tim. "Smell the gray leaf trees?"

Tim's jaw opened. He knocked the brim of his lucky hat a little higher, exposing his wrinkled forehead. As he stepped forward, the ship listed farther. Micah dropped against the wall with a groan.

Tim snapped his gaze away from Bailey and supported his nephew to keep him upright. "We have to get off this ship. Micah, go to the portside tender with the crewmen. I'll delete our navigational data and get the medical supplies then take the starboard tender to meet you on the shore."

"No," Micah protested. "I'm responsible for this vessel. I should be the last one off."

Professor Tim turned to the instrument panel and started flipping switches. "Get to the tender so you aren't hurt any worse than you already are. I'll meet you on the shore with the supplies. Just go!"

Micah looked down at his wounded arm. The lower half was swelling. "Fine. We'll go." He nodded once to his crewmen, and they followed him to one of the ship's two tenders.

Bailey thought of the backpack in her cabin below deck. This morning, she'd packed it with the few possessions she would need if she had to make a quick exit, just as she had as a teen when she suspected she would be shuffled between foster homes without notice. Instead of following Micah and the crewmen to the tender, she took one last look at the misshapen moon then dashed down the narrow steps and pushed open the door to her cabin.

The black waterproof backpack waited for her at the foot of her bed. She checked the compartments: a change of clothes, multi-blade pocketknife, bar of soap, stormproof matches, compass, thermal blanket, hand-crank flashlight, water bottle with filter, binoculars, rain poncho, and the well-worn copy of *The New Testament* her coach gave her in eighth grade. Her hiking shoes were zipped in the shoe compartment at the bottom of the backpack, and the sunglasses she'd taken from Justin Mercer's desk were safely tucked inside the front pocket.

"Land, here I come." She fastened the zippers, strapped on the backpack, and hurried above deck.

The crewmen were readying the tender to be lowered to the water. Micah was already in the small boat, holding his broken arm across his chest. When he saw Bailey, he waved her over with his good hand. "Hurry! We're about to leave."

She held up a finger to him then stepped into the bridge to speak to Professor Tim. "Are you ready to go?"

"Not quite."

"Let me tell the guys to leave and I'll stay with you."

Tim was stuffing a box of syringes into his pack. "My insulin is in my cabin."

"I can get it."

"No, I'll get it. You go with them. I want to know you're safe." He slid a handheld two-way radio into his bag and offered a second radio to her. "Here, put this in your backpack. Micah is in too much pain to be dependable, and I don't trust Armed or Dangerous. Use the radio to contact me once you're on the beach but only if there is an emergency."

"A bigger emergency than being on a sinking ship?"

He chuckled once. "Go! I'll meet you on the shore… on the Land."

"Yes, on the Land. Be safe."

He pointed to the black embroidered giraffe on the side of his white bucket hat. "I'm wearing my lucky hat. I'll be fine."

"Lucky? Some scientist you turned out to be." She flashed him a quick smile then gripped the shoulder straps of her backpack and dashed to the tender.

The two crewmen worked a pulley system to lower the tender into the water. The side of the narrow watercraft thumped against the listing ship as the crewmen sat at either end of it with Micah and Bailey facing each other in the center.

Bailey ran her hand under the plastic seat until she found a life vest. She offered it to Micah.

He shook his head. "If we capsize, I'd swim better without that."

"You only have one useable arm."

When he didn't reply, she held the life vest on her lap and studied the moonlit coastline ahead. "We're not far from shore."

The crewman sitting at the aft revved the outboard motor and guided the boat toward the beach. The other crewman kept one hand on an oar and the other on his holstered gun. Bailey caught his eye. "If this is the Land, the people who live here are peaceful. Don't freak them out with that thing."

He grunted. "And if this isn't your *Land*?"

"It is the Land." Her toes curled inside her rubber reef shoes. "What else could it be?"

The crewman ignored her question. He returned his gaze to the shore ahead of them and kept his hand on his pistol.

Once away from the yacht, the forward momentum of the waves helped to usher the little boat toward the beach.

Though the night blackened the greenery on the shore, Bailey peered at the dark tree line beyond the foreshore. Surely, those were gray leaf trees. Their scent filled her lungs with hope.

Wishing she could discuss the overwhelming aroma with Tim, she looked back at the yacht. It seemed farther away than she expected. The lone emergency light in the bridge was no longer visible. Professor Tim had lowered the other tender to the water. As the waves lifted and lowered in her line of sight, she couldn't see him. Hopefully, he was starting the motor and they would be safely reunited on the shore of the Land within minutes.

She glanced at the Land ahead and said to Micah, "Almost there."

The crewman at the front of the boat skimmed the water's surface with his oar. He yelled to the crewman who was working the motor, "We're in the shallows."

The engine quieted to a stall. Above the sound of water lapping at the sides of the boat, a man's voice carried on the wind. Bailey looked back to see if it was Professor Tim. His tender was a white blur some fifty yards behind them.

The voice called out again. It sounded like it was coming from somewhere in front of her, not behind. She couldn't see any movement on the beach. It was probably her imagination or an animal. She almost reached for the radio Tim had given her, but he'd said not to unless it was an emergency. They were nearly to shore and Tim was headed in the right direction, so this wasn't an emergency.

As the crewmen rowed, one of them said to Micah. "Only twenty meters to go, mate."

Micah's face was stuck in a permanent grimace of pain. "I have a bad feeling about this."

Bailey touched his trembling knee. "Your uncle is coming with the medical supplies. We'll get some painkillers in you and splint your arm. You will feel better in no time."

Micah nodded once, seeming more like an injured yellow belt outmatched on the mat than the fiercely independent yacht captain Bailey had gotten to know over the past few days.

The boat slowed to a stop, and the crewmen poked their oars into the shallow water. The crewman at the bow said, "The bottom is scraping. Walk from here. Bailey, get Micah to dry sand while we drag the boat toward the trees to tie it up."

Bailey stepped out of the boat, and her reef shoes found the shifting sand just below the water's dark surface. Micah refused to be helped out of the boat, but he stayed close to Bailey as the group trudged through the last laps of water to the dry sand. Her joy at having land beneath her feet was stifled by Micah's pain-filled breath. His broken arm needed to be set, and soon.

The boat swished over the sand behind her as the crewmen dragged it by a rope. The full moon shone brightly enough the four of them cast gunmetal-gray shadows on the beach. Above the boat's scratchy noise, the distant male voice called out again.

It wasn't Bailey's imagination.

Someone was close by. If they had landed where Justin Mercer claimed was the only entry point to the Land, the village of Good Springs was a short hike beyond those trees. Bailey held up a hand, pausing the crewmen. "Did you hear that voice?"

The crewmen stopped beside her and Micah. They exchanged a look and reached for their weapons. The rope they used to pull the boat slacked as they glanced around.

Micah said, "Maybe it was my uncle."

Bailey looked back to see the distant yacht. "No, it wasn't Tim." She scanned the dark water for his boat, but it wasn't in sight. "He should have made it to shore by now. Do you think something is wrong?"

Micah squinted. "He's fine. I can see his tender."

"I can't. Where is—"

"Stay where you are!" A man shouted from the shadowed tree line. "Don't move!"

As Bailey turned toward the voice, the crewmen dropped the rope, sidestepped Bailey, and pulled their handguns. "No!" she yelled.

Deafening pops of gunfire pierced the air as the crewmen shot toward the tree line.

The authoritative voice bellowed from the shadows. "Drop your weapons!"

The crewmen fired more, shooting haphazardly into the darkness, their eyes lit with fear and fury.

Bailey began to shout at them again, but Micah pulled her behind himself, shielding her with his body. She neither needed nor wanted his chivalry. As she moved to see around him, she caught a moonlit glimpse of men running between the trees.

Bailey sucked in a breath as something flew past her through the air from the tree line. She reached for the zipper on her backpack to get the radio and warn Tim not to come ashore, but the sharp hisses of ammunition flying made her flinch. No martial arts block would stop a bullet.

Both of the crewmen fell to the sand, motionless. Their gunfire ceased. Long, thin lines protruded from their torsos.

Before Bailey's eyes could focus on the objects, Micah jerked backward, knocking her down. He landed on top of her legs and didn't move. Her left knee popped, and the outside of her thigh stung with a white-hot pain.

The air went silent, except for the hum of the incoming waves. The crewmen didn't move, nor did Micah. Bailey struggled to sit up, her leg pulsing with pain. She scanned the tree line but saw no one.

Micah's head lulled to the side. She reached for him, and her hand hit a long thin bolt that jutted from his ribcage. She tried to pull it out, but its tip was lodged between his ribs. Warm liquid soaked his shirt around the arrow's entry point. Her stinging leg felt wet too.

She yanked herself out from under Micah, and his unconscious body slumped to the sand. "Micah!" she tried to rouse him.

He groaned.

She rose to her knees to lean over him. Her leg burned. She had finished tournaments before with pulled muscles and jammed fingers; surely, she could ignore this pain while she got Tim's nephew to safety. "Micah!"

She reached for his neck to check his pulse but stopped as several people armed with crossbows ran toward her from the trees. One, two, three, four, five of them, all males in their twenties or thirties, aiming their crossbows at her.

This couldn't be Good Springs. Justin had said the people were peaceful—Quaker-like almost. These definitely weren't the Colburn relatives he'd told her about.

The tallest man moved in front of the others and stopped them about ten feet away from Bailey. Moonlight struck his angular face. "Hands where I can see them!" he commanded with a forceful American accent.

Bailey considered every possibility for escape, Tim's probable distance behind them, and whether she could defeat five armed men by herself with an injured leg.

The leader had black hair and a warrior's posture. "Drop your weapon!"

"I don't have a weapon."

"Hands up!"

She raised both hands, her fingers still wet with Micah's blood.

The guy to the leader's left wore a flat-brimmed hat and suspenders. He had frantic eyes that darted from her to Micah and the fallen crewmen and then back to his leader. Shock quaked his deep voice. "It's a woman. She's wearing men's trousers and has short hair, but it's a woman."

The leader didn't care she was female, and he didn't look surprised. He wasn't from here, but maybe the others were. Suspenders Guy definitely wasn't from America, at least not this century.

The leader yelled at her, "Face down on the ground! Now!"

She could disable two maybe three of the men, but not five while they were armed. And what good would come from it if she tried to fight? She would be a fugitive in a foreign land—a land she'd been told was peaceful. Besides, the crewmen had fired first and initiated the fight. Since she was with the crewmen, the locals saw her as the enemy. By the look in their leader's eyes, he would hunt her down if she escaped. And Professor Tim had yet to come ashore. When he did, they might attack him too.

She would comply for now and try to contact Connor Bradshaw. Justin Mercer had assured her his former navy co-pilot was happily living the good life here with the Colburn family. She was supposed to deliver Justin's sunglasses and a note to Connor when she found him.

If she found him.

She lowered her body to the ground and squeezed her eyes shut to keep the sand out while footsteps scurried around her.

"Keep her covered," the leader yelled to his men. His voice grew closer to where Bailey was lying beside Micah. He pulled off her backpack, bending her shoulders unnaturally. "What's in this?"

"Girl stuff."

"Any firearms?"

"No."

One of the locals who stood near the fallen crewmen spoke with a quick clip to his words, and she couldn't place his accent. "This man is shot clean through." Then after a few seconds, "So is this one."

"Take their guns but be careful. Keep them pointed at the ground. Don't touch the trigger," the leader said, as if his men had never handled a gun. Then he squatted beside Micah. "This one is bleeding but still alive. Carry him to the medical cottage. Quickly."

At that, Bailey lifted her head from the ground. Three of the five men were walking away, each carrying one of her wounded and none of them seeming weakened by the task. Now it was just her, the leader, and Suspenders Guy, who looked like he'd never seen blood.

The leader patted her down. "Do you have any weapons?"

"I told you I don't. I'm a scientist."

When his palm hit her stinging thigh, she almost screamed.

The leader motioned to Suspenders Guy. "Help her up. Take her to Lydia too." Then he looked at her. "Don't try anything stupid."

CHAPTER FIVE

After an enjoyable evening of supper and cards with the inn's other guests in the dining hall, Solo walked out to the stables to check on King. Then he retired to his room. He sat at the rolltop writing desk by the south-facing window and pulled off his boots.

Lace curtains trimmed both of his corner room's windows and a full moon's blueish glow made him reluctant to light the chamber lantern on the desk. He leaned into the chair's padded back and looked out across the inn's majestically illuminated property.

From his upstairs view he could see the shadowy roofs of Leonard and Claudia's cottage and the laundry house next door to it. To the left a slice of the bunkhouse was visible behind Leonard's cottage and the side of the big barn blocked the paddock. If he leaned close to the glass, he could see the greenhouse through the big gray leaf tree to the right. He would have to go to the other window for a view of the stone bridge and the road, but he didn't feel like standing up.

The moonlit property awakened his imagination, and even though his eyes wanted to keep staring out the window, stories stirred inside him as strong as the ocean currents around the Land. He had forty days to write, and he didn't intend to waste one of them.

The brown leather satchel his granddad had given him on the first day of secondary school waited atop his wooden trunk. He opened the satchel's leather flap and withdrew the writing paper he'd acquired by trade back home in Riverside. He laid four sharpened pencils on the desk beside the blank paper and opened his notebook.

The first story he'd outlined wasn't his story at all but one his granddad told him when he was a boy. That would be the final story in the children's storybook he was compiling, and he would end the book with a dedication to the man who had taught him the art of storytelling.

The other stories outlined in the notebook were his own creations. They came from a lifetime of days spent alone with the horses and the hills, weeks of travel across the Land, and years of seeing God's truth displayed in nature.

With the strike of a match, he summoned the lantern's wick to life. As he replaced the chimney on the lamp, a soft knock rattled the bedroom door. He quickly hid his notebook in the writing desk's empty drawer. "The door is unlocked."

After a long pause, the knock came again.

Whoever it was, they would have heard him the first time. He trudged to the door and opened it. "Yes?"

Eva stood in the hallway, holding out a folded towel and a washcloth. A day's work had tired her eyes, but it hadn't stolen her beauty. "Sorry to disturb you. Claudia forgot to put towels in the guest rooms today. It was just brought to my attention."

"Thank you." He accepted the soft towels, which still bore the crisp floral scent of laundry soap. When he opened his mouth to say goodnight, she held up a hand.

"Might I have a word with you?"

"Sure." He stepped back and widened the door. "Come in."

"No, thank you." She took a half step forward and stopped at the threshold. "When did you and my father make this deal for a forty-night stay?" Although she spoke coolly, a flare in her gaze gave away her suspicion.

He glanced back at the desk, eager to return to it. His anticipation to write surely outweighed whatever personal qualms the inn's manager had with her father's business arrangement. He started to close the door. "I'm not one to come between family members. If you have a problem with Frederick's decision, you should take it up with him."

She pressed her foot against the door, not allowing him to shut it, but kept her tone professional. "Answer my question, please. When did my father agree to this?"

It didn't matter how she said it, or how pretty her feminine figure looked standing outside his door, she had crossed a line. He'd left his boss behind in Riverside and had come here for peace. The threat of harassment tightened his stomach, so he used the tone he usually reserved for obstinate horses. "Our trade has been in the making for a long time."

"A long time?"

"That's right. Good night, Eva."

"How long?" She didn't remove her foot from the doorframe. "I was never made aware of your paying us any extra trade. Have you kept records?"

He blew out a long breath. "Yes. So has your father. Good night."

"May I see your records?"

"Again, if you have a problem with this arrangement, that is between you and Frederick. I suggest you ask him for his records."

She still didn't back away. "He hasn't been himself lately. His memory is slipping."

"I know. I'm sorry. Good night."

"You knew?" The flare in her eyes grew into a flame. "Is that how you took advantage of him?"

He could have closed the door on her rude behavior and forgotten about it by morning, but being accused of tricking an elderly man out of room and board reminded him of how his brother used to make up accusations to get him into trouble when they were kids. It set his teeth grinding. "I would never do such a thing. You don't know me well, but your father does, and he suggested this deal for reasons that have nothing to do with you or the inn. For the last time, good night, Eva."

The fire in her brown eyes cooled, and all that was left was sadness. Surely, his honesty hadn't grieved her. Whatever the cause, it must have been there before, but he was only seeing it now.

She pressed her lips in a grim line and backed away. "Forgive me, Solomon. Good night."

The latch clicked against the strike plate as he closed the door. He'd never met Eva's late husband, but Ezekiel Vestal must have had nerves of iron to be able to stand such a woman. Solo had come through the inn shortly after Ezekiel's death and remembered the thick sense of tragedy that lurked in the air. The next time he'd stopped at the inn, Eva was holding her infant son, and the following year she was managing the inn with Zeke toddling around in her office.

Solo couldn't imagine the turmoil Eva had endured, losing a husband while carrying his child. All at once, reality hit him like a horse kick to the chest. Even though she appeared to possess the strength to overcome anything, she was still a widowed mother, a sole parent doing the job of two people.

And now with her father's failing memory, she was doing the job of three and fighting to protect her family's business.

Maybe he should tell her the real reason he was here. Surely, she wouldn't mock him for writing children's stories; she was a mother after all. She wasn't the schoolyard bullies who had stolen his journals or the ridiculing ranch boss who refused him a moment of peace to write. He would speak to her first thing tomorrow morning.

He sat at the desk but instead of working on his stories, he blew out the lamp and got lost in the stillness of the moonlit property outside his window.

CHAPTER SIX

The burning pain in Bailey's left thigh tempted her to limp as she took her first few steps on the beach's shell-covered sand. She must have been jabbed by something or pinched a nerve when Micah collapsed on her. The spasm in her quadriceps kept her from being able to diagnose the injury, and she wasn't about to look at it or touch it in front of her captors. It could be deadly to reveal weakness to an opponent. She drew a deep breath and forced her gait to appear as normal as possible.

Suspenders Guy slid Bailey's backpack straps over his shoulder and carried his crossbow in his left hand. He walked beside her with his right hand gently splayed on the middle of her back, more like he was shepherding an errant child than capturing an enemy combatant. The quiver at his side was empty, but his leader was walking a few paces behind them, dragging the little boat. She shouldn't try to take both men down and escape because Micah would need her when he regained consciousness.

The three locals carrying Micah and the crewmen had already disappeared ahead. Bailey glanced back at the ocean once more. Professor Tim was nowhere in sight. The leader followed her line-of-vision to the ocean then raised a dark eyebrow at her. "Keep walking," he commanded.

Pine needles crackled underfoot as Bailey left the beach and entered a path between the trees, Suspenders Guy still touching her back. She almost jerked away, but the overwhelming aroma of the gray leaf filled her lungs. If she'd been welcomed to the Land as warmly as Justin had implied, she would be relaxing with deep inhales of the peace-giving scent and enjoying the details of the terrain. Instead she was trying not to limp while being escorted into captivity by a nineteenth-century plowboy and an American crossbow-wielding five-o.

Towering limbs blocked out most of the moonlight until she exited the forest. Suspenders Guy escorted her along the path through a pasture, past a barn, and toward the back of a Federal-style brick home. Great, she was a prisoner in Colonial Williamsburg. At least Justin Mercer had been right about that part.

Suspenders Guy took his hand off Bailey and pointed at a white two-story cottage near the brick house. He spoke with less angst than he had on the beach, but he still looked shell-shocked. "That's the doctor's office."

The slithering sound of the boat being dragged along the path stopped, and the leader's footsteps grew closer behind Bailey. She didn't have to look back to know he was close enough she could plant a roundhouse kick in his throat if she wanted to. For Micah and Tim's sake, she didn't. But if he got any closer to her heels, her reflexes might engage before her mind had the chance to stop them.

A lamp outside the cottage's open door burned brightly, illuminating the structure's white clapboard and gingerbread shutters. A flatbed farm wagon was parked between the brick house and the cottage. The two horses hitched to the wagon raised their heads to give Bailey a disapproving look then went back to munching the driveway's sparse grass.

As Bailey neared the cottage door, the leader came around the front of Suspenders Guy and stopped him. "Wait out here with her. Don't let her out of your sight."

While the leader stepped inside, Bailey tried to see what was happening in the doctor's crowded office. Three of the locals who'd been at the beach were standing with their backs to the doorway. The lantern light glowed between the men, but Bailey couldn't see past them.

The men's muffled words all had the same quick clip like phonograph recordings of historical American speeches from the late 1800s, except the leader. He spoke with a modern accent. "Revel is outside with the female. She has an injured leg but managed to walk here."

Then a woman's voice said, "Everett, Levi, Nicholas, take these men to the wagon for now. Then, Levi, get Father. He needs to know what's happening."

The leader walked back outside. He glared at Bailey. "Was anyone else on that sinking yacht with you?"

If he'd seen the yacht from the shore and knew it was sinking, how had he not seen both tenders leave it? There was no way she was telling him about Professor Tim. She shook her head.

"Are you sure? We don't want anyone else getting hurt." He stood almost toe-to-toe with Bailey and looked down at her. With Suspenders Guy standing behind her, she felt trapped between them. She almost shoved the leader to get him out of her face, but the other three men stepped out of the cottage one by one, each carrying a body wrapped in a sheet. When the last man passed them, Micah's feet dangled out of the bottom of the sheet.

Bailey sucked in a breath. "He isn't dead!"

"They all are," the leader replied. "The doctor pronounced all three men dead on arrival."

She clenched her fist. It was still sticky with Micah's blood. Those idiot crewmen were to blame. They shouldn't have fired first. She told them not to.

Professor Tim would be devastated. He would blame himself for Micah's death. Tim had lost his wife and sons to the water poisoning. Micah had been his last living relative.

And she had his blood on her.

She lowered her fist and wiped her hand on her thigh, but her jeans were wet as well. His blood must have drenched her leg when he landed on her. She'd been too overwhelmed by the firefight to realize how badly he was hurt.

The horses never raised their heads from the grass while the local men loaded Micah and the crewmen's bodies onto the wagon. She couldn't let them cart off her dead. Professor Tim would want to say goodbye to his nephew. She had to stop them.

She tried to sidestep the leader, but he moved quickly and stayed in front of her. She tried again. He lifted a hand to stop her, but she knocked it away before he could touch her.

His nostrils flared. "Do not test me. I won't let you hurt these people."

"I'm not going to hurt them."

With his eyes still on her, he pointed his chin at the cottage doorway. "You need to have the doctor look at your leg." Then he said to Suspenders Guy, "Take her inside and stay with her, Revel."

She fixed her gaze on the three white bundles lying inert on the back of the wagon. She'd brought those men to the Land. This was her fault. A gentle tug pulled on her elbow.

The man called Revel escorted her into the cottage. He lowered her backpack to the floor by a narrow staircase then took off his flat-brimmed hat and motioned with it, his voice hoarse with suppressed emotion. "This is our doctor."

A woman in her mid-twenties wearing a white blouse and long blue skirt stood in the center of the wood floor. She smoothed her light brown hair, tucking a loose strand into her bun. She looked like she'd just walked out of a frontier library, if there even was such a thing. "Right, well," she pressed a hand to her middle. "Let's have a look at your injury."

Bailey took a hesitant step forward, and Revel didn't follow her. He closed the door, sealing them into the doctor's office, then leaned his hand on a ladder-back chair beside a neatly arranged writing desk.

The doctor pointed at a cot behind her. "Lie down there, please."

A rumpled wool blanket covered the cot's mattress. One of the three men had been lying on it when the doctor had pronounced him dead just moments ago. Maybe it had been Micah.

"No, thanks," Bailey answered, wanting to open the door. "I can stand."

"Please, have a seat."

"I'm fine."

The doctor pointed at Bailey's thigh. "You are not fine."

Bailey looked down at her jeans. The once faded blue fabric was now soaked in a wide swath of dark red liquid. "It's not my blood. It's Micah's."

"Micah," the physician repeated on a breath, as if putting a name with one of the men she probably considered heinous invaders made him more human. "Your trousers are ripped." She stepped to the desk and picked up the smallest of the three oil lanterns burning in the room. She held it near Bailey's jeans. "Your leg is lacerated. It's still bleeding."

Bailey touched the rip in her jeans. Her thigh muscle jumped when her fingers contacted the torn flesh. "Oh."

"Come, lie on your right side."

Bailey looked at Revel, and he glanced away. Neither of them saw her as a threat even though she'd been with the men who had opened fire. Probably because she was a woman. Big mistake. Their clothes and houses weren't the only proof that a bygone era was still alive in the Land.

As Bailey took a step toward the cot, the doctor touched her with a compassionate hand. All at once, she couldn't block out the pain any longer. With one kind touch from a caring woman, Bailey's guise weakened. Her blood-drenched leg refused to bend. She limped to the cot and moaned when she sat.

The doctor placed the lantern on a doily-covered table beside the cot then knelt and examined the wound. "You took a deep graze."

"Graze? From one of the arrows?"

"You will need gray leaf medicine immediately."

"Gray leaf medicine?"

The doctor nodded. "It will remove your pain, speed healing, and prevent infection."

Bailey remembered what Justin had told her about his experience in the Land and how the gray leaf medicine cured him of tuberculosis. She let her hands relax onto the cot. "Okay."

The doctor looked up at her and raised a thin brow.

The door opened, snapping Bailey's attention from the doctor. A young woman with similar prairie girl clothes and a blond chignon stepped into the office. She closed the door behind her.

The doctor glanced back at the blond woman briefly. "Sophia, we will need that gray leaf tea after all. This patient…" She looked at Bailey. "What is your name?"

"Bailey—" She stopped before saying her last name. These people might recognize the Colburn name, and she wasn't ready for more chaos.

The doctor continued talking to the woman she called Sophia. "Bailey sustained an arrow wound and needs gray leaf tea."

The young woman backed out the door obediently. "Yes, ma'am."

When the door closed again, the doctor stepped to a cabinet on the wall over a counter between the cot and the desk. "Revel, kindly wait outside for now, please."

"But—"

"I know what you were told to do, but this is my office and my patient needs privacy."

Revel flopped his hat onto his sweaty head and frowned. He glanced from Bailey to the doctor and back to Bailey. "If you need me, I'll be right outside the door."

Bailey wasn't sure which of them he was talking to. He'd looked at her when he spoke, but why would she need him?

The doctor drew a clear jar from the cabinet. She shook its dried gray leaves into a stone mortar. "Do you want to remove your trousers or shall I cut them?"

Bailey bent down to peel off her sand-caked reef shoes. The pain in her leg intensified. Some of the blood was drying and gluing the denim fabric to her skin. She wanted to take her pants off but didn't want to sit in her underwear while strangers traipsed in and out of the doctor's office. "Just cut them. I have another pair of jeans in my backpack."

"Jeans," the doctor repeated in the same faint way she'd repeated Micah's name.

"Yes, jeans. Pants made of denim."

"Oh, yes of course." The doctor ground the leaves with a pestle then returned to the cot with a pair of silver sheers. Her touch was light but confident as she cut away the material, leaving Bailey with only one pants leg. After pouring water into a ceramic basin, the doctor washed the area around Bailey's wound with a wet cloth. "The arrow cut deeper than skin."

Bailey sat up to look at her injured leg.

"No, lie back, please." The doctor left the bloody cloth in the basin and stepped back to her cabinet. "After you drink the gray leaf tea, I will clean the wound, then coat it with salve and dress it."

"How long is this going to take?"

"Not long. Your pain will be gone soon. Lie back, please."

Bailey complied and stared at the dark wooden beams in the ceiling. She had to get back to the beach and find

Professor Tim. Not that the leader here would make it easy for her. The doctor had disregarded the leader's command to Revel. Maybe Bailey could get the doctor on her side. She raised herself onto her elbows. "What's your name, doctor?"

"Lydia Bradshaw."

"Bradshaw?" She remembered Justin's co-pilot's name. As she opened her mouth to ask Dr. Bradshaw if she knew Connor Bradshaw, the door opened.

Sophia stepped inside, holding a steaming kettle. Revel was standing outside the door as he'd said he would. He closed the door behind the doctor's young assistant. His remorseful eyes met Bailey's before the door closed.

Dr. Bradshaw poured the steaming water over a tea strainer, and the gray leaf's potent aroma filled the room just like it did when Bailey was analyzing the saplings Justin had raised from the seeds he'd procured in the Land. She was in the right place, and if Dr. Bradshaw knew Connor, she was close to finding the right people. But she was being held prisoner, Tim was missing, and the others were dead.

Dr. Bradshaw returned to the cot and offered Bailey a porcelain cup of the steaming tea. "Drink this, then lie back. The effects of the gray leaf tea can be quite overwhelming."

CHAPTER SEVEN

Eva stepped away from Solo's closed door feeling like she had swallowed a brick. So maybe he hadn't taken advantage of her father's failing memory when he made this deal, but he was still taking advantage of the inn. This house was supposed to be a place of rest for weary travelers, not a long-term destination for boorish horse breeders. Didn't he have a job at a ranch in Riverside to get back to?

She delivered the last set of guest towels then walked to the other half of the house where her family's rooms were. She passed Sybil's door and almost knocked. It would be so nice to stay up late talking like they did when they were younger—long before Revel left and their mother left and their other brother James left, long before the sad truth set in that half of their family was gone and their world would never be the same. But it was half past ten now. Sybil would be sound asleep. She would be awake at five in the morning and be happy to talk while she started her work in the kitchen, but there was no way Eva was getting up that early. Six came too soon as it was.

Eva walked to the end of the hall. Her parent's room was on the right. It was really just her father's room now, but they all pretended along with her mother that she would return to the inn when her elderly parents passed away and her duty with them was fulfilled. She wouldn't. She'd always struggled with being out here in the middle of the Land, away from village life.

Turning the knob as quietly as possible, Eva opened her door and peeked in at Zeke, who was curled up under his red blanket on the double bed they shared. He was big enough to need his own bed and would soon need his own room. The thought of him being in a separate room at night added dismay to the ever-growing pit in her stomach. What if he died in his sleep like Ezekiel did? The doctor had said the heart condition that killed him was probably something he'd been born with. What if Zeke had inherited that defect?

Before she went back downstairs to turn out the lights for the night, she had to make sure Zeke was breathing. She tiptoed in—bypassing the one squeaky floorboard—and glimpsed his sweet face, relaxed and cherub-like. Of course, he was breathing. He was fine, just like he was fine when she checked on him an hour ago.

The white and brown puppy Solo had given Zeke was curled up on an old blanket on the floor by Zeke's side of the bed. The dog raised its head at Eva, and she backed out of the room before it fully roused.

Downstairs, the lamps had been extinguished in the kitchen and dining hall. One wall sconce was still burning in the reception room, so she turned its knob to kill the flame. The only lights still burning were a sconce in the hallway and the lamp in her office. Expecting the room to be empty, she jolted at the sight of her father sitting at her desk. He looked up at her with bloodshot eyes. "Hello, Peach."

"Father. What are you doing up... and in here?"

His gruff voice was barely above a whisper. "It's still my inn, isn't it?"

"Of course." She leaned against the edge of her desk. Maybe posturing herself above him physically would empower her, even if she had no real authority here. "I came down to close up for the night."

"Heard you up there knocking on guest room doors."

"Claudia forgot to put towels in the rooms again."

He yawned but managed to point a crooked finger at her. "Don't talk bad about your elders."

"I'm not. She has too much to do. We all do."

He scratched his chin through the thick white whiskers of his beard. "Tomorrow at breakfast I'll find out if any of the traders are heading to Good Springs and send them with a message for Revel. It's time he came home."

She looked away, wishing she didn't have to tell him about the letter she'd received. "Revel isn't coming home. He should, but he isn't. He is happily living his own life. So is James." When her father's expression drooped, she decided there was no sense in mincing words now. "We need more workers. If you don't hire men or let me hire them, we will have to start turning away guests. Especially if you're going to give away forty-night stays to horse breeders. We can't handle extra burdens."

"Solomon Cotter isn't a burden. He is paying for his board, fair and square. You'll treat him like any other paying guest."

This was pointless. Why did she try to reason with her father? He only ever listened to her if she was doing exactly what he said or expected. Who knew what he expected of her now. Maybe to run the inn and pick up all the slack since the aging farmer, aging stable manager, and aging housekeeper could no longer keep up with their chores. She used to tell herself her father would soon see the error of not taking her recommendations, but the more his mind slipped, the less he could see reason. "It's time for bed," she said as she turned out the chamber lantern. The only light in the room came from the hallway sconce and the moonlight coming through the windowpanes.

Frederick pushed himself out of the chair with a grunt then stood wobbling for a moment as he got his knees to hold his weight. "You're right, Peach."

At least he agreed with her that it was time for bed. She turned and walked to the office threshold, waiting to close the door behind him. When she turned back to look at him, he was still standing by the desk.

He leaned his knuckles onto the desk's paper-covered surface. "You are right." His voice held a sadness that made her regret being annoyed with him.

She crossed the rug and touched his back. "Come on, Father. I'll take you upstairs."

He patted her hand but didn't look at her. "They aren't coming back. None of them. It's just you and me and Sybil. My knees pain me so and the gray leaf medicine does nothing for them. I need another man to take over the stables soon. I can't wait the years it will take for Zeke to grow up. And… my cousin…" He snapped his fingers impatiently. "What's his name?"

"Leonard."

"Thank you. Leonard needs less work, not more. His back hurts him so badly he can hardly stand upright. We have to hire some help."

Though he said the words Eva had been desperate to hear, a lump rose in her throat. She didn't want her father to be too old to work, too old to remember what he was doing. The silence between them called for her to respond, but her jaw clenched on emotion, so she waited. If she cried in front of him, it would make things harder.

He stroked his beard. "I guess this is what I get for marrying a woman twenty years my junior. When I was ready to settle into my golden years, she was still young and wanted to go back to her village." He turned his face toward her then but still didn't look her in the eyes. "As for Revel, well I don't know what got into that boy. He knows the tradition. He knows he should come back here and take over his inheritance." His voice quaked. "It's fine for James to take a job shepherding the Fosters' flock in Good Springs; he's my second son. But not Revel. No firstborn son should ignore his family obligations like this."

The shock of hearing her father speak ill of Revel squeezed her already heavy heart. "I'm so sorry, Father."

He patted her hand again. "It's not yours to be sorry for, Peach. You've done more than most daughters would for their family." He cleared his throat then looked at her. "If you find a man or two I would approve of, hire them."

CHAPTER EIGHT

Steam mixed with the sharp gray leaf scent and rose from the teacup as Bailey lifted it to her lips. She sipped slowly at first, testing the tea's temperature. Its taste matched its aroma, which was rich and slightly bitter, reminding her of mint and earth and eucalyptus. It was unlike anything she'd ever tasted. With each sip she wanted more. Her sips turned to gulps, and the teacup was soon empty.

Dr. Bradshaw held out a hand to take the teacup. Bailey passed it to her and started to speak, but before she could say anything, her diaphragm jolted, forcing her to inhale audibly through her mouth. Fire rose in her belly as the gray leaf tea swirled with the bile and the fear and the regret inside her. The heat radiated from her core down to her legs, dissolving the pain in her wounded flesh, and then up to her heart, her arms and neck, and finally to her head. Specks of light darted through her vision, blurring everything—the doctor's caring expression, the quaint medical office, the silhouette of the man who stood guard outside, the reasons why she'd come to the Land, the shock over the death of the crew, the barrage of all that she'd lost…

Her mind froze on that thought.

She'd lost Tim to the waves, lost her mother to prison, and lost earning her degree to the world war. Gone was her chance to get a job as a plant biologist and make enough money to buy a house far from the city like the one she'd briefly lived in with a foster family when she was ten.

Sentiment swirled inside her along with the gray leaf tea. She had to get ahold of herself. Professor Tim was out there somewhere, and he needed her as much as she needed him. Without him she was a lone survivor, a wounded prisoner, a desperate defector of a world in chaos.

White streaks fuzzed her eyesight, ruining her ability to focus. Maybe this was all a bad dream. Maybe she was sleeping in her private cabin on the yacht, floating on the sea where a peaceful land was rumored to exist. Maybe she'd never left the Unified States and was still in her plant-filled apartment in the pigsty of post-World War Three Norfolk, Virginia.

Despite the surreal light affecting her vision, she scanned the rustic furniture in the medical office, the old-fashioned attire of the doctor, the perfectly clear water in the pitcher on the counter. This was real. She was in the Land. She'd risked her neck to find the one place left on earth with enough space and water and food to support the life she dreamed of. Somehow, she'd made it here.

The beams in the ceiling moved above her. She must have rested her head on the cot at some point, but she didn't remember lying back. Gentle hands touched her leg and the calm voices of the doctor and her assistant filled her mind.

Dr. Bradshaw applied a layer of salve on the wound. It didn't hurt. Not only could Bailey not feel pain, she couldn't remember what pain felt like.

She wished Tim were here so he too could witness the miracle of the gray leaf. He was probably wandering up and down the beach with his lucky hat on, trying to figure out where Bailey and the crew had gone. Maybe he would follow their footprints through the trees. The path led directly to the doctor's office. Maybe he'd knock on the door at any moment.

Logic fought the serene apathy created by the gray leaf medicine. If Tim approached the cottage while Revel and the other goons waited outside, they'd probably tie him up. Or lock him up. But why? Tim had done nothing wrong. Nor had she. Maybe the locals would treat him fairly. Come to think of it, they weren't mistreating her. She watched the doctor and her assistant as they dressed her wound.

Maybe Tim would make it here okay and Revel would let him inside the doctor's office. The two-way radio was in her backpack, which had gotten pushed under the chair by the desk. If the women left the room at some point, she could call Tim over the radio and report everything.

Dr. Bradshaw was busy at the supply cabinet, so Bailey curled her finger at the doctor's assistant, drawing her closer. "Sophia, was it?"

"Yes?"

"Is it normal for the gray leaf medicine to cause confusion?"

The young woman crinkled her flawless brow and glanced at the doctor, whose back was to them as she cleaned medical instruments on the counter beneath the supply cabinet. Sophia looked back at Bailey and shrugged. "I've never had to drink it, but I'm told it promotes a deep sense of calm in most patients."

"I'll say." A hum buzzed Bailey's throat, and for a moment she thought someone else had made the noise. She almost laughed. "I should be freaking out, but everything seems fine even though I know it's not. I'm calm but confused… but I'm also okay with it. But not."

Sophia and Dr. Bradshaw exchanged an amused glance, and then the doctor lifted the basin of blood-tainted water and said to Sophia. "I'll dump this in the pit. Stay here with her."

"Yes, ma'am."

Revel peeked in at Bailey while the door was open. She tried to meet his gaze, but her vision doubled. The door closed behind the doctor, and Bailey's head felt lighter by the second. Her breathing slowed along with her heart rate. If she was going to pass out, she had to secure the radio unit. She reached for Sophia's hand. "My backpack…"

Sophia pointed at something across the room as if deciphering Bailey's slurred speech. "Do you want your bag?"

"Yes, but not now. I need you to do something for me."

Sophia pulled her hand away and arched one honey-toned eyebrow. "What?"

"Not anything bad. Just watch my stuff for me if I fall asleep, okay?"

Sophia stared blankly.

Bailey's tongue felt like it was growing inside her mouth. She struggled to speak clearly. "Look, I'm a private person. You get it, right?"

"Get what?"

"There isn't anything valuable in my bag, but it's all I have left in the world. Don't let anyone take it, please."

"No one here would take your things, ma'am."

"Ma'am? I can't be that much older than you."

"Pardon?"

"Never mind." The blithe feeling produced by the gray leaf made her want to laugh, but her voice wouldn't create the sound. She cleared her throat. "I'm sorry. You have manners. It's nice. I'm glad I'm in the Land even if you people aren't the peace-loving Quakers that Justin Mercer made you out to be. Not that it matters to me right now. They shot me with an arrow, but this is still better than living out there."

As her eyes closed, she realized what she'd said. Hopefully her words had been as undecipherable to Sophia as they felt in her mouth. She looked up at Sophia. "I'm sorry. It's the gray leaf medicine, I guess."

"I understand."

Yes, the doctor's assistant did seem like an understanding young woman. She willed her voice to stay strong so she could get as much information out of Sophia as she could while Dr. Bradshaw was outside. "Tell me, am I in a village called Good Springs?"

"Yes," the young woman whispered even though they were the only people in the office. The color drained from her rosy cheeks. "A moment ago… did you say Justin Mercer?"

"Yes. Did you meet him while he was here last year?"

"No, but Dr. Bradshaw did. He was Connor's co-pilot in the outside world."

"Connor?" Bailey struggled to open her heavy eyelids. "You know Connor Bradshaw? Where is he? It's urgent that I find him. Once I explain everything, he will get me out of this mess. I need to meet him, pronto!"

Sophia took a cautious step backward. "You already met him. He was in charge of the security team that was training this evening when you and your men invaded the shore."

As Sophia's words sank in, Bailey tried to raise herself from the cot. Her body refused to move. The heat from the gray leaf pulsed through her veins. The room disappeared, and silence filled her mind.

CHAPTER NINE

The first glow of daylight turned the eastern horizon the color of lilac blossoms as Solo walked out to the stables. He knocked the brim of his hat higher to take in the exquisite morning sky. The last pinpricks of starlight faded softly to the west. From the inn's elevated land, the surrounding hills' varied shades rolled all the way to the gray leaf forest in the east. This was perfect country if ever he'd seen such a thing.

A steady ribbon of smoke rose from the laundry house's chimney. Claudia must be getting an early start on her work. A trader padded from the bunkhouse to the shower shed with a half-asleep expression on his face and a towel over his shoulder. No matter which direction the man would be traveling from the inn, he had a full day on the road ahead of him.

Solo rolled open the tall doors at the stable's arched entryway, sending a nervous lizard scurrying for the rocks. He latched the doors to keep them open for the day the way Frederick always did. It was odd the stable manager wasn't already here. He used to have the stalls mucked out before breakfast.

Solo stepped inside the stable block where the musky scent of hay and horse manure filled the morning air, just as God intended. King whinnied to him from the back stall. "I'm coming, boy." He grabbed a lead line from a peg on the wall outside King's stall and opened the door. "Come on. Let's get you to the grass."

King compliantly marched behind Solo through the palatially-sized stable block. The ranch back in Riverside was the biggest operation in the village, and it didn't have buildings like this. There was room in here to drive a wagon through the center and still have space to spare.

Outside, the sun peeked over the eastern hills, casting the fence's shadow in a long grid pattern across the dewy grass. Solo unlatched the gate and led King into the paddock. The feeder buckets nailed to the fence posts were empty.

He removed King's rope and gave the stallion a pat. "You'll have to settle for grass until I can talk to Frederick about the oat feed." The horse was already munching on the low grass, content with what he had.

As Solo returned to the stables to check on the two mares that he'd bred with King last April, Leonard lumbered out of one of the other horse stalls, leading a dun gelding. The thin older man's shoulders were rounded forward and his upper back was humped. He nodded stiffly. "Morning, Solo."

"Good morning, sir."

"Going to be a fine day."

"Indeed."

Leonard pointed at the stalls on the opposite side on the stables. "Both of those mares are close to foaling."

"I was just about to check them."

"I'd give Sadie two more days, but Star will be ready sooner. Probably today."

Solo grabbed a brush from a rack on the wall and stepped into Sadie's stall. The dapple gray mare took a step backward and shook her mane. Solo offered her a handful of hay. Her lips wet his skin as she ate from his hand.

"You remember me, don't you Miss Sadie." He brushed her as he slowly walked around her and looked for signs of labor. Her pendulous abdomen and waxing teats confirmed Leonard's assessment.

Solo finished brushing Sadie then walked to the next stall where Star was pacing in circles and swishing her brown tail. When Solo stepped into her stall, the bay mare paused briefly and gave him a don't-you-dare look. He stayed where he was and watched her stomp the dirt floor. She turned her rump toward him, and her tail swished far enough to the side to give him all the information he needed.

He backed out of the stall while Leonard was walking past, now leading a second horse as well. "You were right. Star is in the first stage of labor."

Leonard and his two horses stopped at the same time. The older man looked in at Star, turning his whole body as if his neck was too stiff to twist. "Going to have a foal walking around here real soon, aren't you, girl?"

Star ignored him and kept up her restless pacing.

Solo pointed a thumb to where the feed was kept in a storage room at the west side of the L-shaped stable block. "What time does Frederick come out to feed his horses?"

Leonard glanced toward the open archway. "He hasn't come out before breakfast for a while now."

"Which is at what—seven?"

He nodded and the loose skin beneath his chin wobbled. "Lately, while the traders are eating, Eva makes her rounds to each table, asking if anyone can stay an extra day and help out. Every day but Sundays. Most of the time a couple of the men will be able to stay. One will clean stalls and tend to the horses in here while the other helps me with the farming."

Solo studied Leonard's weathered face. Tight lines creased his brow and sun spots marred his nose and cheeks, but he had clear, gentle eyes that reminded Solo of his granddad. He looked back at the mares' stalls. "Once these foals are born, I'll help out where I can."

"That's right gracious of you. Eva would probably be most appreciative too."

He thought of his heated spat with Eva at his door last night—his aggravation and her fiery insolence. "I'm not so sure."

A quick grin lit Leonard's face then slowly melted away. "Don't worry about Eva. She's tough because she has to be tough. Been through a lot. Sees this place as hers to look after until her big brother comes back. And now with her daddy getting like he is…"

Solo remembered what his parents had gone through when his granddad's memory failed. With Frederick being almost two generations older than his adult children, the change must have come as a shock to them. "How long has this been going on?"

Leonard raised an eyebrow. "Our getting old? Awhile now." He chuckled at his own joke.

"No sir, I meant—"

"I know what you meant. It's just hard to think about." One of the horses behind Leonard snorted impatiently, and he either ignored it or didn't hear it. "Most days Fred does all right. He has moments where he doesn't know what's happening or where he is, but he snaps back in no time. His knees pain him too, usually in the mornings. He does less and less work every week, which is normal for older folks."

"How are you holding up, if you don't mind my asking? Aren't you close to his age?"

Leonard pulled back his head. "Not close at all. Fred's seventy-two; I'm only sixty-eight." He winked, reminding Solo even more of his granddad. "Even though my back tries to keep me down, I still milk the cows before dawn and can put in a full day in the fields." He looked down. "But not Fred. He can't get on a horse anymore."

Solo glanced out the high archway at the slice of the inn that was visible from where he stood. He'd planned to assist with the mares' foaling then spend the rest of his time here writing. He would need to write during all thirty-nine of his remaining days at the inn if he was going to finish the storybook, take it to the printer in Good Springs, and return to his job in Riverside by mid-May like he'd promised when he left without much explanation. His boss had assumed it was about family trouble, and Solo hadn't corrected him.

Now, there was a need before him that had nothing to do with his own family or his desire to make them proud by carrying on his late granddad's storytelling tradition. But he couldn't sit in his room imagining heroic adventures while these good people struggled with stable work and farm chores. He'd just have to write late at night or work faster to finish the farm work early.

Either way, it would make his project even more challenging. Still, right was right. He put a hand on Leonard's shoulder. "I'm staying here for a few weeks, and while I'm here, I'll help out all I can."

CHAPTER TEN

Blurry slivers of golden light pried Bailey's tired eyes open. She pulled the lumpy pillow out from under her head and flopped it on top of her face. Was today a school day? Coach was determined to send her to Nationals, so she probably had another early morning practice.

The blanket covering her skin itched. Wool. Ugh. A different foster house every few months meant beggars couldn't complain. Something was weird about this bed though. She would have remembered falling asleep with a wool blanket.

As she rolled over and licked her chapped lips, the taste of gray leaf tea sparked her memory. Every detail of her entrance to the Land flooded back at once. She yanked the pillow off her face and sat up.

An orange sunrise tinted the gauzy curtains that covered both windows across from the cot. The door between the windows was closed. Was Revel still standing guard outside?

She was alone in the doctor's office. Where was— what's her name—Sophia? Where was Dr. Bradshaw for that matter? The doctor had to be Connor Bradshaw's wife. Sophia had said Connor Bradshaw was the leader of the group of men who had been at the shore. That explained his American accent and military demeanor.

Sophia had also called the men a *security team.* No wonder they shot back when the crewmen opened fire. They were defending their village. She would have too.

Still, Micah didn't deserve to die; he'd been unarmed. And so had she, yet the very man who Justin had said would be her ally in the Land had ordered her to be taken prisoner. So much for having someone she could trust here.

She needed to find Professor Tim before Connor Bradshaw and his security team did. The gray leaf tea might have knocked her out for a night—at least she hoped it had only been one night—but she wasn't debilitated.

Lowering her feet to the cold wooden floor, she wiggled her toes. Her body seemed functional. She peeled the bandage and gauze from her thigh to check the wound. Instead of raw flesh, there was shiny, pink scar tissue. The gray leaf had healed her while she slept.

She stood and stretched her arms high overhead, moving slowly out of habit since an old dislocation injury had left her with a limited range of motion in one shoulder. Both arms rose symmetrically. She reached behind her, swooping each arm in a wide circle. The once-restricted arm moved as freely as the other. The gray leaf medicine had healed an old injury too.

She wanted to know more about the gray leaf tree. The bottles, beakers, and open notebooks on the counter below the doctor's supply cabinet beckoned her. Since the day Justin Mercer introduced her to his gray leaf saplings, her scientific mind had raced with the healing potential of the unclassifiable plant. Now she'd come to the Land—the only place on earth where the gray leaf tree grew—and had experienced its miraculous effects.

But she hadn't come to the Land alone. The man who'd taught her plant biology was somewhere on the shore. And right now, he didn't need her scientific mind; he needed her survivalist's determination.

Footsteps creaked the floorboards upstairs. Someone else was in the cottage. Bailey tiptoed across the office and knelt by her backpack, which was still tucked under the chair beside the desk. Upstairs, water ran in a steady pour. Whoever was up there must be taking a shower.

Hoping she had time to change out of her one-legged pants, she drew a fresh pair of jeans from the backpack's main compartment. The radio was nestled inside just as she'd packed it when Tim gave it to her on the yacht. She turned it on but kept the volume on the lowest setting while she quickly dressed. White noise hummed from the speaker.

She unzipped the compartment at the bottom of the backpack and pulled out her hiking shoes. Once they were laced tightly, she shook the sand out of her reef booties and tucked them inside the empty compartment.

The water stopped running upstairs, but the boards only squeaked in one area of the ceiling. Her warden was still in the bathroom. For a prison they were fairly lax. At least no one had taken her backpack during the night, just as Sophia had promised.

Bailey held the radio close to her ear. Nothing but static. She pressed the talk button, and the static stopped. "Professor Tim? Timothy Van Buskirk? Can you hear me?"

She released the button and waited for a response. Silence. After clearing her dry throat, she tried again. "Tim, if you can hear me, please respond."

Still nothing.

She turned off the radio then flipped out its hand crank mechanism and spun it for a minute to charge the battery. She would try to contact Professor Tim again once she was on the beach.

Water ran upstairs once more, making her thirsty. A pewter jug and cup sat on the bedside table. She strapped on her backpack over her Eastern Shore University sweatshirt, then poured a cup of water. The cool, clear liquid was the first drink of pure water she'd swallowed since the water poisoning that started the war. She emptied the cup with deep quaffs then refilled it. No foul stench, no salty remnants of filtered seawater, just pure freshwater.

After filling the bottle in her backpack, she walked to the door. The running water stopped upstairs and so did the footsteps. She glanced up the staircase but only saw a closed door at the top. Whoever it was, they weren't worried about her escaping.

She peeled back the sheer curtain that covered the window by the door. No one was outside. A door to the big brick house was only a few yards away. An impressive array of azalea and hydrangea shrubs lined the back of the house. If she wasn't trying to flee, she would have walked straight over to examine the beautiful specimens.

The wagon that had been parked between the house and cottage was gone now. The men must have taken the bodies somewhere during the night. Micah's body. She had to find Professor Tim and be the person to tell him his nephew was dead. He shouldn't hear the news from strangers.

Turning the knob as quietly as possible, she opened the door and peeked outside. All clear. A cow mooed in the distance. She stepped into the misty morning air and carefully closed the door behind her. Before the latch clicked, a voice came from the big house. "Miss Bailey, I presume."

A middle-aged man stood in the back doorway. Shadows darkened the tall figure, but as he stepped outside, the morning light hit him, illuminating his gray hair and blue eyes. The smell of freshly baked muffins wafted out of the big house, making her stomach rumble.

The man tilted his head. "She said you were sleeping."

"Who?"

"My daughter, Dr. Bradshaw." He glanced back into the house then walked toward Bailey, leaving the door open. "We thought you were still recuperating from your injury."

Bailey let go of the cottage's doorknob. Should she run? Where? To the beach? Then what?

The older guy stopped walking midway between the house and the cottage. He didn't seem threatened by her, and he certainly wasn't a threat to her. Her leg wound was healed, she'd regained the range of motion in her shoulder, and the long drink of pure water had refreshed her system. She could dodge him and take off if she had to. "I was injured, yes, but the gray leaf medicine helped." She hooked her thumbs in her backpack straps. "I have to go now."

"Where?" he asked, advancing another step.

Bailey glanced in both directions. To the west, the dirt tracks of the driveway led to a road about a hundred yards in front of the house. The path she'd walked from the beach last night disappeared to the east. She couldn't see what was on the other side of the cottage, but from the animal sounds, she guessed a farm. "To wherever they took my crew. I need to see them."

The man pressed his lips together. "You cannot see them."

"Why not?"

He lowered his volume. "Last night, we buried your men in our cemetery behind the village chapel."

"So quickly? Maybe they weren't dead. Did you even check?"

"My daughter is a thorough physician."

Bailey touched her scarred leg. He was right.

And he wasn't treating her like a prisoner. She stepped forward. "You're Dr. Bradshaw's father, right?"

He nodded once and offered a hand to shake. "Reverend John Colburn. I am the overseer of Good Springs."

She considered his waiting hand. They shared ancestral roots, and she'd come here to meet this family. More than to meet them, she wanted to connect with them. She shook his hand. "I'm Bailey." She paused a beat, wondering if she should say her last name and acknowledge they shared an ancestry. Her stomach growled, ending the silence awkwardly.

He lowered his chin and compassion filled his crystalline eyes. "Would you like some breakfast, Miss Bailey?"

Maybe she should eat before she went to search for Tim. No. She'd work better if an empty stomach drove her. She didn't need food as much as she needed information. If John Colburn was as easygoing as he appeared, maybe she could confirm some details from the doctor's father. "No, thanks. Tell me, is your daughter married to Connor Bradshaw?"

He released her hand. "Yes. Are you acquainted with Connor?"

"No. Not personally. It's a long story."

John stepped around her and opened the door to the cottage. "I have plenty of time."

When he motioned for her to step inside the medical office, she glanced back at the path that led to the shore. "I don't."

"Are there more coming? More men with guns?"

A baby's happy squeal sang from the big house. Dr. Bradshaw appeared in the doorway, holding a toddler on her hip. "Oh, you're up. Sophia said you were still sleeping. She went upstairs to take a shower."

Dr. Bradshaw smoothed the toddler's black hair. The little boy had the same dark eyes as the security team's leader. Bailey didn't want to see those eyes again until she'd located Professor Tim. She held up a palm to John. "I can't stay."

Dr. Bradshaw walked closer. "But your leg. I'll need to check the wound before I release you from my care."

"It's fine, really. Thank you for your help. I should go."

John opened the cottage door wider. "It's not that simple, Miss Bailey. The last person who came here from the outside world was very sick and spread the illness to my youngest daughter. If you care about the welfare of my people, allow Lydia to complete her examination. Then you may leave my property."

His calm authority commanded Bailey's respect. She didn't have an infectious disease, but they were entitled to their procedures. And yes, she cared about his people. After all, some of them were her people too.

She gave the path to the shore one last scan then stepped back inside the medical cottage. The door at the top of the staircase opened, and Sophia bounded down the steps. The fringe of her puffy bun was curled with dampness. "I'm sorry. I thought you were still asleep."

John put a hand to Sophia's shoulder. "If you would kindly tend to Andrew for the morning."

"Yes, of course," the young woman smiled as she walked to Dr. Bradshaw and took the baby.

The doctor kissed the little boy's cheek and passed him off to Sophia, then followed John into the office. She pointed at the unmade cot, just as she had the night before. "Take a seat, please."

Bailey kept her backpack on and sat on the rumpled wool blanket which was still warm with her body heat. John folded his arms and watched solemnly as Dr. Bradshaw asked questions about Bailey's health and symptoms. While the doctor listened to Bailey's heart and lungs, the seriousness of coming to the Land sank in. These people were isolated from the rest of humanity, and she'd just walked into their world as if it were a national park, as if she had as much right to be here as anyone.

Only she didn't.

She came here on a tip from an untrustworthy man who'd once brought disease to these innocent people. She wasn't like Justin Mercer, nor was she like the crewmen who'd stood on the shore blindly firing bullets at the locals. She'd come here to partake in the simple and safe life these people had spent generations building. But now everything was ruined.

Dr. Bradshaw and John and Sophia had treated her with kindness even though they were probably terrified of her and of the threat she posed to the Land. Their land. They deserved the truth.

Bailey caught the doctor's eye. "I'm not sick. I never had the plague—the disease Justin Mercer was sick with when he came here." At the mention of Justin's name, Dr. Bradshaw and John exchanged a look, but Bailey continued. "I lost all of my friends to it though. All except one: my former professor, Timothy Van Buskirk. He didn't make it to the shore with us last night, and I need to find him. He's sick, but his disease isn't contagious. He's diabetic. If he doesn't have his medicine with him, he will probably need your gray leaf tea soon."

Dr. Bradshaw walked to her desk and began writing with a silver pen on a thick piece of grayish paper.

John stepped closer to Bailey. "How many others are coming?"

"It's only Tim, and he isn't armed. It was just the five of us on the yacht that sank last night. And the two guys who had guns were crewmen I barely knew." She felt like she was defending herself to the school principal. "It was Micah's yacht. Tim's nephew. He was unarmed. He didn't deserve to be shot. He was doing Tim a favor by bringing us here."

John angled his head. "That is the problem when strangers arrive on foreign soil shooting at the men who are training to protect their people. I am grateful to the Lord that none of our men were killed by your armed crewmen."

She started to say she was sorry, but John continued with an authoritative tone. "Our security team spent last night patrolling the beach, expecting more men to come ashore."

"Did they find Tim?"

He shook his head. "Three of my men went home to their families at daybreak, but Connor and Revel stayed at the shore."

She stood up. "I need to go too."

"If your friend came ashore, Connor and Revel will find him."

"I need to be there when they do."

He cast a quick gaze at Dr. Bradshaw. "I will not keep you here if the doctor says you are healthy."

Dr. Bradshaw set her pen down. "She is healthy, but I don't think it's wise for her to go to the shore while Connor is… in his current state of mind."

Bailey waited for an explanation, but none came. "I can defend myself."

John raised a hand, stopping her. "Miss Bailey, we do not want you to have to defend yourself. We prefer peace."

"So do I. That's why I came to the Land. Justin said this is the only peaceful place left on earth."

"Yes, but the way you and your men arrived last night gave Connor a different impression. If you insist upon going to the shore, I will go with you."

CHAPTER ELEVEN

Eva sat in the cushioned chair at her desk in her quiet office but couldn't relax. The morning sun reflected off a shiny porcelain vase by the window. It sent splinters of blinding light into her eyes. The pearlescent vase with gold trim had been a gift from her mother when Eva turned sixteen. She looked out the window to where the iron bench waited beneath the tall gray leaf tree. Instead of closing the curtain on her view of Ezekiel's final resting place, she moved the glossy vase out of the direct sunlight.

Her gaze was drawn to the shaded area in front of the bench where her late husband's headstone hid in the grass. She quickly snapped her focus back to the desk. There was too much work to be wasting time staring out the window.

She rummaged through a stack of papers until she found the recommendation letter for Isaac Owens, the man from Southpoint. As she reread it in preparation for Mr. Owens' interview, Claudia stopped in the hallway outside the open office door.

The older woman shifted a bundle of kitchen towels in her arms and blew a wisp of silver hair off her sensibly thin face. "Which rooms need sheets today, dear?"

Eva scanned the reservation book. "Only Rooms Two and Three. Mr. Owens from Southpoint is staying again tonight. He is helping Leonard cut hay today."

"Oh, yes. Isaac Owens. Nice young man." She lowered her volume and grinned a little. "Fine to look at too."

"Actually," Eva held up the recommendation letter and waved Claudia into the office. "I might hire him permanently."

Claudia's eyes widened, flattening the creases at their edges. "Does your father know?"

Eva nodded. "He gave me permission last night. He finally acknowledged it's time." She drew in a breath of the triumphant air that still floated in her office. "At last, I can secure the help we need around here. Things are about to change."

Claudia's grin receded, and she tightened her hold on the dirty laundry as if clinging to a branch over a flooded stream. "What are you saying, dear? You aren't sending Leonard and I away, are you?"

"No, never. You and Leonard are a part of this inn and always will be. More than that: you are a part of this family." She smiled, trying to ameliorate the fear in Claudia's eyes. "It's just that... since Revel isn't planning to come back, I must hire men for the stable manager and farm manager jobs."

Claudia was still suffocating the laundry bundle. "But one of those jobs is my husband's livelihood."

Eva held up a hand. "Leonard will still be in charge of the farm as long as he wants to be, and you both can live in the cottage for the rest of your lives, even when you're no longer able to work at all. This property is your home as much as it is mine. I simply need to find our new farm and stable managers… for Father's sake and for Leonard's. I spoke with Leonard this morning, and he agrees it's for the best."

Claudia dabbed the sweat from her cheek with her shoulder. "Yes, his back makes it difficult for him to work."

"As Father's knees do him." Eva stood. "I've been praying for a solution, and Father finally came to his senses. Once I hire the right man, Leonard will have permanent, reliable help. And hopefully soon I'll find someone to take over the stables for Father."

Claudia nodded. "I'm sure you will. By the way, this Isaac Owens isn't married. I already checked." She wiggled her silver eyebrows. "On the other hand, if your new stable man has a wife who would like to take over the laundry, I won't be offended." Her expression lightened. "Course, if you hire men who are unattached, maybe one of them would make a good companion."

Eva almost groaned. "For whom?"

Zeke squeezed around Claudia in the doorway, holding his puppy. She lifted her chin at Zeke. "For little Zeke… but mostly for you."

Eva shook her head rapidly hoping that would end the conversation before Zeke's curiosity was roused.

Claudia flashed a quick smile then walked away to take the bundle of dirty rags to the laundry house.

Zeke didn't look like he was paying attention to what Claudia had hinted at. He looked up at Eva. "Are you getting someone new to move here?"

"That's the plan."

"Who?"

"Just a couple of men to help out Grandpa and Leonard."

"What about Solo? I really like him. Can he live here always?"

"No, sweetie. He's only staying forty days." Though she still didn't know why exactly. He was impossible to get answers out of, and she had more important things to tend to. She glanced at her reservation book and mumbled. "Thirty-nine days now."

Zeke held up the little white and brown spotted dog. "Grandpa said Joshua can go with me while I go clean out a horse stall."

It was one thing to allow a six-year-old boy to follow the men and help out with easy tasks, but giving him the chore of cleaning a horse stall by himself might be too much. She'd go out to the stables after her interview with Isaac and make sure Zeke was all right. "Very well." She petted the puppy's soft head. "Keep Joshua away from the horses."

Zeke dashed to the side door before Eva had finished her sentence. "I will," he yelled as the screen door slammed.

Eva sat again at her desk and found the supply list under her reservation book. She would mention the inn's need of lantern fuel, rope, and chicken wire to the traders who were leaving today. Most of them were good about bringing whatever supplies the inn needed the next time they came through.

Footsteps creaked the upstairs floorboards as guests prepared to leave or go work outside for the day. Isaac Owens should be coming down soon. Eva was eager to speak with him, eager to secure her first hire.

Water swished and dishes clanked in the kitchen as Sybil cleaned up from breakfast. As soon as the interview with Isaac was over, Eva would check on Zeke then do a quick pantry inventory with Sybil before she spoke with the traders.

And there was something else she was supposed to do this morning. What was it? She blew out a long breath as she realized she'd sent Zeke out to the stables for the day without making him do his school lesson first. She would keep him inside after lunch and read to him.

The busyness of the inn was both her nectar and her noose. She needed this place as much as it needed her. Though her father had given her the authority she craved, everything inside her screamed for quiet. But whenever it was quiet, the clattering beat of her lonely heart was more unsettling than the chaos of a busy day.

Claudia had hinted that Eva needed a companion, and Sybil had said the same thing at dinner last night. By *companion* they weren't speaking of a friend but of a husband. That was out of the question. Her companions were her family and the guests—even if half of her family had left the inn and the guests were usually gruff traders and weary travelers who provided her little true companionship.

She'd had her one constant companion in Ezekiel, her first and only love, though it was only for a few months. Still, when she said *forever*, she meant it.

Isaac Owens knocked on the doorframe as he stepped into the office. He had a fuzzy light brown beard trimmed short like his hair, one ear slightly smaller than the other, and a smile that could melt stone. "Miss Roberts?"

Eva stood and opened a hand to the armless side chair by her desk. "Please, have a seat. It's Mrs. Vestal, actually. Mr. Vestal is no longer with us. You may call me Eva."

Isaac sat on the edge of the chair and threaded the brim of his hat between his fingers. "I beg your pardon. I didn't know."

"That's quite all right. My husband passed away a long time ago." She sat and picked up the letter from Isaac's last employer. "You haven't been in the trading business long, have you?"

"No ma'am. Only four months."

"Not taking to it?"

He shook his head. "Not like I thought I would. I promised my boss to stay on until he finds someone else."

She'd hoped whoever she hired would be able to start immediately. "Yes, that's admirable."

Isaac continued, "I am ready to go back to farming. That's what I'm good at."

She pointed her pencil at the letter. "So Mr. Ashton of Southpoint says." She read part of the recommendation letter aloud. "Isaac Owens was the best farmhand in my employ. He is hardworking, honest, and has a keen sense of the land."

Isaac pressed his lips together reverently. "He was very generous."

"Why not go back to work for him then?"

A sadness darkened his eyes. "Southpoint isn't the best place for me."

Her mother couldn't wait to get back to Southpoint and this man didn't want to return. He seemed too young to have a past. She set the letter aside. "How old are you, Isaac?"

"Twenty-five last week."

He was only a year younger than her, but she felt twice her age most days. He was a grown man and deserved privacy about his past as much as she did hers. "We're close in age, you and I. However, my father is over seventy. He and Leonard both have difficulty with their work now. Leonard has severe back pain, but he forces his body to keep going. You will see what I mean while you work with him today."

Isaac nodded. "He told me all about the farming operation here, and it wouldn't be too much for me to manage. In fact," he straightened his posture, "I have a few ideas for how to increase production."

She held up a hand. "I'll leave that between you and Leonard. If you are hired, Leonard will still have a say in how the farm operates."

"Yes, ma'am. That's fair. I'm ready to work with him." His enthusiasm was like a fresh breeze blowing across the hills in summer.

She hoped he still felt as eager after spending a day working with Leonard. "Do you have any questions about the job or the inn?"

He pointed up. "Would I be living in a guest room upstairs or the farmer's cottage?"

"Upstairs until we could build you a place. The cottage belongs to Leonard and Claudia. Leonard is my father's first cousin. He moved out here from Riverside when Father inherited the inn."

Isaac nodded then looked at the floor while he thought. After a few seconds he said, "I guess that's all. Do you have any questions for me?"

She studied his young face. Surely, he had a life somewhere. "Would you be comfortable living this far from the villages? Wouldn't miss home or a sweetheart or anything?"

He grinned. "I prefer country life and I don't have a sweetheart."

Sybil dropped something in the kitchen, and the clink of metal hitting the floor echoed across the hall.

Isaac turned his face toward the sound. "The food here is the best I've tasted. Who is the cook?"

"My sister, Sybil."

"Sybil," he repeated softly as if her name held magical powers. He kept his gaze on the hallway a moment longer. "Yes, I reckon living here would suit me fine."

Life at the inn might suit him, but a day with Leonard in the fields would prove whether he suited them. It was far from final, but the possibility of having the first position filled almost made her sing. She kept her joy tamped and offered her hand. "Excellent. Work with Leonard today. We'll talk more this evening."

CHAPTER TWELVE

Bailey climbed an outcrop of volcanic rock and scanned the shore. Seagulls crowded the beach, some running along the sand, some dive-bombing the shallows. The tide had erased Bailey's footprints from last night, along with the prints of Micah, the crewmen, and the tender they had dragged onto the beach. The men's bodies had been buried hastily in a cemetery Bailey had never seen, and even their marks in the sand were gone. Now the hard-packed beach was corrupted only by two fresh sets of men's boot prints and thousands of bird tracks.

Bailey looked down at John from her rocky perch. She had to raise her voice above the squawking gulls. "I thought you said Connor and Revel were here now."

"They must have taken the path through the village back to my house."

She wanted to contact Tim on the radio but remembered Justin saying all electronics had been banned here. Connor feared generating signals would make the Land detectable to the outside world. There was no way Bailey was letting her two-way radio get confiscated. She fished her binoculars out of the pack's side pocket instead.

The thick foliage of gray leaf trees, pines, and hemlocks followed the shore northward until it faded into the horizon. To the south, the outcroppings multiplied until they blended into rocky bluffs that rose high above the ocean. Violent waves crashed against the cliffs, spraying foam and mist into the air.

She lowered her binoculars. "How far did your men search last night?"

"From the bluffs," he swooped a hand from the south toward the north, "up to Weathermon's Point."

"Maybe Tim heard the gunfire from his boat and turned back to the sea." Through the binoculars she searched the ocean's surface. The morning sun reflected off the water in blinding rays. "If he doesn't know it's safe to come ashore, he might be staying out there on purpose."

John scratched his trimmed gray beard and glanced around. "Connor had his telescope when he and Revel came back here this morning. Since there are only two sets of footprints leaving the beach, they must not have found your friend."

A thought hit her like a sucker punch. "Or they apprehended Tim and carted him back to the village like a dangerous criminal." She shoved the binoculars into her backpack and hurried down from the rocks. "We have to go back to your house."

"Connor and Revel are both fair men. They would not—"

"They don't know Tim is harmless. He's a scientist and a kind man." Her words poured out on stunted breath. "And he might not feel well."

John put a hand on her shoulder. "Try to calm down, Miss Bailey."

She jerked away from him and walked a tight circle in the sand, reminding herself more of a pouting brat than a world-ranked fighter. Something about John made her feel like a child in need of comfort. She stopped in front of him. "You don't understand. Tim lost his family during the water poisoning. I lost all of my friends, my coach, everybody. Everybody but Professor Tim. He made this journey possible for me because he wanted me to meet my... to have a better life. I don't have any family at all. Tim is my only friend. I can't lose him too."

John lowered his chin and studied her intently. He was quiet for a moment, as if choosing his words delicately. "We will do everything we can to find your friend."

She swallowed the emotion from her outburst. "Thank you."

He raised a finger. "But you should know the currents are violent around the Land. If your friend has not come ashore yet, it is unlikely he will. You would be wise to prepare yourself for any outcome, Miss Bailey."

Something in the gentle way he spoke made her want to fall into his arms and weep like a lost little girl. It would be foolish to depend on someone she'd just met, even if she'd already given him a glimpse of her feelings. She hadn't meant to. This was no time to let down her guard. She didn't know John Colburn. So what if they were related?

So everything.

The only reason she'd destroyed Justin's gray leaf saplings and his proof of the Land's existence was to protect these relatives she'd never met. Tim had encouraged her to find the Land for the very purpose of connecting with others who shared her Colburn roots. Now the patriarch of that family stood before her and she was holding back.

She turned her face a degree so the ocean wind would hit her square on and keep her hair out of her eyes. "Listen, it's not *Miss Bailey*. I know you're being polite, but Bailey isn't my last name; it's my first. My name is Bailey Colburn."

His eyes rounded, showing white above the blue. "Colburn?"

"I'm a botanist from Accomack County, Virginia. Justin Mercer hired me for a research job with the gray leaf saplings from the seeds you gave him. He chose me because he discovered I'm a descendant of the same Colburn family that you are."

"How exactly?"

"My fifth great-grandfather was George Colburn, the brother of William Colburn, your ancestor who settled here. Justin thought my being related to you would make me trustworthy about the Land's existence."

John drew his head back. "Mr. Mercer swore he would take the secret of the Land to his grave. Many of the men on our elder council doubted his sincerity. I left it in God's capable hands." He went quiet for a few seconds then a faint grin lightened his expression. "And you were mistaken."

"I am?"

"You said you don't have any family at all. It appears as though you do." He stepped away from the rocks. "Come, have some breakfast, Bailey."

Looking at the vacant shoreline tightened her chest. "It doesn't feel right to leave here and go have breakfast while Tim is still missing."

John nodded. "We will tell the others about your friend and form a search party but not on empty stomachs. Come."

Bailey walked beside John along the sandy path through the forest. He pointed out a pile of stacked stones, saying it was a cairn erected in 1861 when the founders arrived in the Land. As they exited the forest, he pointed to a flagstone with a C engraved in the center. "This marks my property's bounds. This was my father's property before me and his father's before him and so forth for generations. It is our tradition that the firstborn son inherits his father's property and profession."

"What if the firstborn is a girl?"

He shook his head. "Our founders established the traditions to provide order."

"Sounds misogynistic."

"I believe there is wisdom in our traditions, but many here have made other choices. My son included." He looked up at the big brick house as he spoke. "But with God's help, we came to an agreement."

When they reached the house, the back door was still open. The aroma of blueberry muffins welcomed Bailey as she followed John into the warm kitchen.

Dr. Bradshaw stood in front of a baby's high chair. She was in the middle of picking up her toddler when she noticed Bailey. She froze for a moment, and the baby's legs dangled over the high chair's crumb-covered tray. Connor and Revel were sitting at a long wooden table near a stone fireplace.

Connor's gaze shot up at Bailey. His cheek bulged from the bite of food he'd just taken. He slowly rose while chewing his food. Revel dabbed his lips with his napkin then glanced at Connor and stood too, as if it were the custom. Connor's vicious glare left no doubt he wasn't standing out of old-fashioned manners.

Though Bailey was tempted to match Connor's stare and see who might blink first, she shifted her gaze to acknowledge his suspenders-wearing comrade. As soon as her eyes met Revel's, he looked down at the table.

Connor threw John a glower. "What is *she* doing here?"

"The same as the rest of us." John maintained a friendly tone as he stepped in front of Bailey and pulled a chair out for her. "She is having breakfast at my table."

Dr. Bradshaw plunked the baby on her hip and pointed at a wide doorway to the next room. "Connor, may I see you in the parlor for a moment?"

Connor kept his suspicious stare on Bailey. "Lydia, take Andrew upstairs."

Bailey didn't need to be treated this way. "I'm not going to hurt your kid."

Connor cocked his head. "You had no right to come to the Land."

"Neither did you."

John raised his voice slightly. "Enough!" When the room fell quiet, he looked at his daughter. "Lydia, you may take Andrew upstairs if you need to attend to him, but he is not in any danger here. Everyone else, sit."

Revel dropped into his seat.

Bailey obeyed John because it was his house and because she could easily pop out of the chair and escape if she had to. She lowered her backpack to the floor but kept one hand on its strap as she sat on the edge of the ladder-back chair.

Connor waited until Bailey sat then grudgingly lowered himself to his seat.

Lydia watched Connor for a moment with concerned eyes then left the kitchen, the baby babbling happily as if all the excitement in the house was fun.

John picked up a breadbasket and offered it to Bailey. A stack of blueberry muffins filled one side of the basket and thick slices of iced pumpkin bread covered the other. She glanced at John and when he nodded once at her, she took a muffin.

Revel stood so quickly his chair screeched on the floor. All eyes followed him as he walked to a cabinet beside a double-basin sink and drew out a ceramic plate. He took a pewter cup from another shelf and placed them in front of Bailey. Then, he slid a milk jug closer to her and a bowl of boiled eggs.

"Thanks," she said as he returned to his seat.

Connor shook his head at Revel.

Revel shrugged in response.

They both turned their attention to John as if waiting for his lead.

John selected a piece of pumpkin bread from the basket and cut a bite with the side of his fork. "I believe formal introductions might put some of this animosity to rest. Bailey, meet my son-in-law, Connor Bradshaw, and our houseguest, Revel Roberts. Connor and Revel, meet Bailey Colburn." He pointed his fork at Bailey. "She is my long-lost cousin."

Connor raised his black eyebrows. "You have to be kidding me."

"Not at all," John answered then quickly returned to his introductions. "Bailey, you already know Connor is from your country, came to the Land four years ago when he was ejected from his aircraft, and is now married to my daughter Lydia. What you might not know is that Connor has made it his mission to keep the Land safely hidden from the outside world. He has proven his abilities and leadership to such a degree that our village elders have agreed he should train to one day take my place as Good Springs' overseer."

Bailey almost snorted. This guy with the belligerent stare? He was going to have John Colburn's job someday?

Then John faced Connor, occasionally allowing his gaze to shift to Revel. "Bailey is a botanist from Virginia. Mr. Mercer hired her to help him with the gray leaf seeds we sent with him to America."

Connor's nostrils flared. He opened his mouth like a protest was clambering to get out, but he stopped short of speaking as John continued.

"Mr. Mercer chose Bailey to help him because he discovered she shares my family lineage. He thought that meant she would be trustworthy."

Connor sneered at her. "Well, you certainly showed him, didn't you?"

If it weren't for John's kind hospitality, Bailey would have reached across the table and ripped the arrogance off Connor's face. Instead, she glared at him. "What's that supposed to mean?"

"Mercer trusted you, and you brought men to our shore with guns drawn."

She shouldn't let Connor get to her. He was the one who'd been prancing around in the dark, teaching the locals how to shoot to kill. If he was going to ignore the fact that she wasn't armed, she was going to ignore him. She turned her attention to Revel, but when he immediately looked down at the table, she shifted her gaze back to John. At least one man here knew how to listen. "Justin Mercer hired me to take care of the gray leaf saplings he'd grown from the seeds you gave him. He wanted a full molecular analysis so he could take it to the military in hopes of regaining his job status. I was the only person he showed the gray leaf to. When I realized the plant was unclassifiable and demanded to know where it was from, he told me about the Land and how my relatives ran aground here in the eighteen sixties.

"His gray leaf saplings were dying. I tried to save them, but Justin said he would have to lead the military here to the Land to get mature trees. He wanted to use the gray leaf medicine to make the Unified States a world power again so it wouldn't join Global.

"I couldn't let that happen. So, I told Professor Tim about the gray leaf tree because I needed his help to save the Land. We stole the saplings and destroyed them along with Justin's data. I thought Justin would come after me. I wasn't afraid of him, but Tim suggested we try to find the Land ourselves.

"He contacted his nephew, Micah, who operated a charter yacht company out of South Africa before the war. Micah only does humanitarian runs out to Tristan da Cunah now." She looked at Connor. "He did, anyway, before you and your goons killed him."

Connor didn't have a quick rebuttal this time. The disdain in his eyes lessened. He leaned forward, listening.

John's hands were calmly folded.

Revel's gaze hadn't left the table. Either he wasn't very bright or the firefight had left him shell-shocked.

She reached down into the front pocket of her backpack and took out the sunglasses case that contained the dark aviators and the note from Justin. "Anyway, Micah agreed to take Tim and me to the coordinates I'd stolen from Justin's data. He hired two guys to come with us in case we ran into trouble. On our way out to the coordinates, I found this in my bag." She held the sunglasses case out to Connor. He opened it and stared, expressionless, at the aviator sunglasses inside.

She passed the folded slip of paper to John. "He wrote me this note."

John read Justin's note aloud: "Bailey, I knew you would do the right thing even though I couldn't. If you make it to the Land, give these sunglasses to Connor Bradshaw. Yeah, I knew you wouldn't be able to resist if I left them on my desk. You can't keep them. They belong to Connor. Tell him all the evidence of the Land has been destroyed, and I will make sure the Land stays hidden. Take care of yourself, beautiful. The rest is up to you. J.M."

Connor closed the sunglasses case, leaving the aviators inside it. The sarcasm had left his voice. "Even though Mercer doesn't have any evidence of the gray leaf tree or the Land now, he will always pose a threat to us. He can't be trusted."

John passed the note back to Bailey. She folded it and tucked it into her jeans pocket. "Justin said no one could detect the gray leaf without the information on its molecular structure. With the saplings and data destroyed, I don't see how he could prove the Land exists."

Connor shook his head. "He could give the military the Land's coordinates and the time to arrive, like he told you."

Bailey doubted that would benefit Mercer. "The military thinks he's crazy. Nobody listened to him. And they definitely won't without proof."

Revel spoke up for the first time, drawing everyone's attention. "Is that all it takes to come to the Land? Knowing where to be and when?"

Connor rubbed both hands across his face. "Apparently."

John wagged a finger. "There is more to it than that. Our founders believed God controls who enters the Land and who does not. Ships have crossed these waters for hundreds of years, and until the *Providence* ran aground, no one had set foot on the Land." He put a hand on Connor's shoulder. "When you first arrived in the Land, you said you had flown over this area many times and never saw any land here. While you were brought to our shore, Mr. Mercer was carried out to sea and lost sight of the Land."

Connor touched the sunglasses case. "But he found it three years later, entered, and safely left after a month."

"Precisely. Because it was God's plan that Mr. Mercer tell Bailey Colburn of Virginia about this place." John put his other hand on Bailey's shoulder as if bridging the feuding parties. "And she found her way here to us."

John left his hands on both of them for a long moment. The muscles in Bailey's shoulders relaxed for the first time in years. Connor's expression softened slightly.

When John removed his hands, he folded them on the table. "Bailey has a friend named Timothy…" He gave Bailey a quizzical glance.

"Van Buskirk."

"Timothy Van Buskirk. He helped her destroy Mr. Mercer's evidence of the Land and was on the yacht last night but did not make it to shore. He is unarmed and a peaceful man. He has an illness that requires medication, and Bailey fears for his life." He looked back and forth between Connor and Revel, including them both in his command. "Form a search party. If Mr. Van Buskirk made it to the Land, we must find him immediately."

CHAPTER THIRTEEN

Solo lifted and lowered the handle on the water pump beside the stable block until cool water flowed out of the iron pipe. He washed his hands and arms up to his elbows then poked the toes of his boots into the flow to rinse them too.

The happy voice of young Zeke echoed off the stable wall as the boy ran from the inn with his puppy scurrying behind him. "Solo! Solo! Mama's coming to see the foal!"

Solo ran his wet hands through his hair before putting his hat back on. He stepped off the well's wooden platform and met Zeke in front of the stable's archway. The puppy yapped excitedly and jumped on Solo's legs. He took a step back and didn't pet the dog so he would go to his new owner instead.

Zeke huffed as he spoke. "I told Mama about Star's foal, and she said she'll be right out to see it."

Solo tousled Zeke's hair. "Sounds good. But after this visit we need to leave Star and her foal alone for the afternoon, all right?"

"Yes, sir."

Eva stepped around the back of the inn and walked briskly toward the stables. Her dark blue skirt flapped behind her like the flag of a pirate ship. When she got close, Solo gave a curt nod of greeting and walked ahead of them to Star's stall.

Zeke prattled all the way through the barn. "I saw the whole thing, Mama. At first Star was lying down, and then she stood up, and the foal was coming out in a white sack, and it took a really, really long time. Then the bag fell out with the foal inside, and Star chewed the bag open and licked the foal to clean it. It was really, really messy." He made a face, and Eva smiled at him.

Solo stopped in front of the stall gate. He looked at Zeke and put a finger to his lips. Zeke mimicked the motion and stopped talking. The little boy stood on his tiptoes, trying to see over the closed bottom section of the stall gate. Solo hoisted him up to give him a better view of Star and her foal.

Eva looked at Solo, and for a moment he thought she was going to tell him to put her son down, but instead she smiled and mouthed, "Thank you."

As Eva watched the foal and Star, she put her hand over her heart and sighed. She tilted her head to one side, and a shiny strand of her brown hair fell across her cheek. Solo didn't want to be caught staring at her, but her awe over the horses' sacred moment captivated him. After only witnessing her tyranny, seeing her tenderness broadsided him like an unforeseen horse kick.

He stood at the gate, holding Zeke up, furtively watching Eva, and wondering why a beautiful, hardworking woman like her hadn't been snatched up by some smooth-talking trader. She glanced at him and raised one perfectly arched brow, reminding him of the accusation she'd made at his door last night. If she acted that way toward most men, it was no wonder she hadn't found a new husband. Maybe he'd been the only man to get a glimpse of what was beneath her rock hard facade.

Zeke's puppy danced around the boy's dangling feet. The dog barked one excited yap, and Star whinnied a warning to them.

Solo lowered Zeke to the ground. "It's time to give Star and her baby some space."

"Yes," Eva said, looking at her son. "And it's time for you to go inside for your reading lesson."

Zeke's face puckered. "Do I have to?"

"Yes, you have to."

Solo nudged him and pointed at the puppy. "You know, dogs love to hear their owners read aloud."

Zeke widened his eyes. "Is that true?"

"Sure is. Dogs love stories," Solo said as they walked out of the stable block. "And since Joshua is just getting to know you, if you read to him a lot, it'll help him learn your voice and feel more at home here."

"Then I'll start right now!" Zeke took off for the inn, and the puppy chased him.

Eva walked a few unhurried steps beside Solo. "I've never seen him get excited to read. Thank you."

"You're welcome." It was the first time they'd been alone since she was at his door last night. He'd closed his guest room door on her, certain she wouldn't let the matter rest. Though her demeanor was different now, he didn't want to risk another argument. She walked toward the house, so he turned to go back into the stable block.

She stopped walking. "About last night…"

He'd almost escaped. Why couldn't she leave well enough alone? A frustrated breath released from his lungs a little louder than he'd intended.

A brief squint betrayed her offense, but she immediately composed herself. "I'm sorry if I was rude. You are a guest here, and I shouldn't have made you feel uncomfortable."

Uncomfortable? She'd falsely accused him of taking advantage of her father's senility, which amounted to saying he had no honor. This wasn't a matter of comfort but justice. But if he'd learned one thing in the schoolyard, it was that forceful people like Eva didn't understand justice; they only understood getting their way. It didn't matter how pretty she was, he wasn't giving her what she wanted. Without speaking, he took a step toward the stables.

She touched his arm, halting him. "I know I upset you last night, and I'm sorry."

He looked down at the slender fingers touching his forearm then at her dark brown eyes. "I didn't trick your father. I wouldn't do that."

"I know," she answered quickly, but her sincere gaze held his. She moved her hand away, and he briefly wished she hadn't. "Anyway, thank you for encouraging Zeke to read." She pointed a thumb at the inn. "I'd better go make sure he's holding the book right side up."

A surprised chuckle rumbled his throat. Where he'd expected an argument, she'd given an apology and charm. There was more to Eva Vestal than he'd imagined, and it pulled him stronger than a dozen Shire stallions. He was tempted to follow her to the house or to invite her to go for a ride or to make her a ring out of a piece of hay.

Somehow, he managed to keep his desire in check and simply tipped his hat to her. "Afternoon."

She smiled politely and walked away.

He stepped into the stable block but stayed in the shadow of the archway, watching Eva as she sauntered to the house.

CHAPTER FOURTEEN

Bailey stumbled out of the botany lab at Eastern Shore University, and a Global officer locked the door behind her. As she limped away, she almost stepped in a puddle then stopped short when she noticed a face in the water.

At first, it looked like her reflection, but a cold wind rippled the water's surface. The image didn't move. She crouched with her hiking boots at the water's edge and studied the person below. The reflection wasn't her face but similar. Her mother? Couldn't be. She died in jail long ago. Bailey got a better look. Yes, it was her biological mother. Twenty-three years since she'd last seen her, and the woman hadn't aged.

Then the face changed, and it was her martial arts instructor. What was Coach doing under the water? Before she could figure out what was happening, the face morphed into Mrs. Polk, her favorite foster parent, and then it was Professor Tim.

"Tim!" Bailey cried.

His eyes opened and focused sharply on her for one desperate second. His mouth didn't move, but she heard his voice. "You can make a family out of friends." Then the image disappeared.

Bailey sat up, panting. She wasn't back in Virginia; she was in the spare bedroom in John Colburn's house in the Land.

She reached to the lamp on the bedside table and felt for the switch before she remembered there was no electricity here. She didn't need light anyway. The bright, oval moon shone through the window sheers.

Standing, she straightened the old-fashioned nightgown Lydia had given her, then she tiptoed to the wardrobe. John had insisted she use it for her clothes. The wardrobe's ornately carved door creaked as it opened. Its interior smelled like lavender and old lady, which were basically the same smell.

Her fingers found the two-way radio in her backpack. She carried it to the window and stood between a wooden rocking chair and a doily-covered side table. The modern electronic devise looked as out-of-place as she felt.

She opened the curtain and let the moonlight hit the radio's digital clock display. 06:18. The clocks on the yacht had been set to Cape Town time, so it was probably an hour earlier here. Maybe two. She could check the Colburns' clock in the living room and set the radio to match it while no one was up to see her. Later. It wasn't knowing the time that had woken her.

She sat in the rocking chair and switched on the radio, trying not to wonder about the deceased relative who had once lived in this room. The look on Lydia's face when she'd shown Bailey to the room told her the death had been recent and the grief still fresh. Bailey knew the feeling well and knew how to bury it even better.

The two-way radio buzzed to life. Static hummed from the speaker on the same lonely frequency as her heart. Her shins ached after spending all of yesterday hiking up and down the rocky shore, searching for any sign of Tim. John had been true to his word and enlisted several village men to help with the search, but they'd found no sign of Tim.

So here she sat by the moonlit window in an old lady rocking chair, wearing an old lady nightgown, hoping to hear Tim's voice over the radio, imagining him curled up in the boat with his lucky hat, lost and hungry. She may have come to a patriarchal society, but she couldn't sit like a helpless female of times past.

She turned the hand crank on the radio for a couple minutes to recharge the battery then switched it off and tucked it into her backpack. After changing into a sweatshirt and her only good pair of jeans, she slipped the backpack's straps over her shoulders and reached for the glass knob on the bedroom door. Something about the way the moonlight caught the smooth knob stopped her. She glanced back at the room where she'd left the bed unmade and the nightgown crumpled on the handwoven rug.

The Colburns might lead simple looking lives, but that was no reason to be a jerk. She wasn't above them. Her technologically advanced society had disintegrated. So what if her people could send a message around the world in a microsecond? Those messages were usually selfish, untrue, or divisive.

She smoothed the bed's soft sheets, spread the warm quilt evenly over the mattress, and fluffed the feather pillows. More care had gone into weaving those sheets and sewing that quilt and stuffing those pillows than into anything she owned. No matter what modern superiority complex had been ground into her psyche, she would show gratitude for the way of life in the Land.

After all, she'd long dreamed of a sweet and simple life.

Now she had the chance to build that life. All that was missing was the man who'd given her this opportunity. She would find him. He was the closest person she had to family. He'd even said himself a person can make a family out of friends, and that's what they'd done. Without him she was alone to face these strangers.

She closed the bedroom door then stepped lightly through the hall and rounded the corner into the living room. The short hand of the clock on the wall behind an overstuffed armchair pointed to V. Five in the morning. She could be at the shore by first light.

As she walked through the wide doorway from the living room to the kitchen, a shadowy figure moved near the stove. Even in the dark, the lines of Revel's suspenders made stripes down the back of his shirt. He struck a match and lit an oil lantern but kept the flame low.

She stepped into the kitchen, and he snapped his face toward her as if she'd startled him. "Why are you up so early?" he asked.

She walked to the cabinet where she'd seen him get a cup for her yesterday. As she filled it at the sink, she avoided answering his question. "I've only been here two days, and on both days, someone was surprised to see me awake the next morning."

A half-smile briefly curved his lips then disappeared as he quickly looked away.

She took a long drink of the crisp water. There was no need to hide what she was doing. "I'm going to the shore to look for Tim. What are you doing up?"

Revel held up a copper kettle. "I wanted an early start."

"Why?" After the word slipped out, she realized work started early in an agrarian culture. She should be more sensitive so she could fit in here. "Sorry. You have chores to do. I get it. I'm not a morning person."

"Nor am I." Revel set the kettle on the stove then walked close enough she could clearly see his features in the dim light. Brown whiskers shadowed his jaw. Faint lines at the corners of his eyes placed him in his thirties, late twenties if he spent most of his time in the sun.

He kept his voice quiet. "I couldn't sleep. Just kept thinking of what happened the other night." His eyes finally met hers. "I'm sorry about your friends."

She couldn't mourn over Micah and the crewmen, whom she barely knew, while Tim was still floating along the coast in the tender. She shrugged, needing to appear tougher than she felt. "Yeah, well, they weren't my friends. Tim was my only friend on that yacht, and he's still out there. I'll find him today."

Revel took a mug down from the cupboard but kept his gaze on her. "Connor said violence is a part of life in the outside world. I can't imagine going through something like the other night over and over again."

She hadn't thought about the trauma the crewmen's violence might have inflicted on Connor's security team. If the locals had never experienced an attack, they were probably in shock. Connor might know how to handle post-traumatic stress, but a person raised in the Land might not. She offered her old coach's words to Revel. "Survivors find ways to cope."

"You are a survivor." Revel's statement came out more like a question.

"Always have been."

"How do you cope?"

She flashed a quick smile, like that would lighten his dark mood. "I do the next thing."

His gaze intensified as if he wanted to say something but couldn't. Just when she thought he was done with their conversation, he shook his head slowly, loosening the strands of sun-bleached hair across his forehead. "It still must be difficult."

She began to deny it, but her ability to pretend was weakening. "Yeah, it stinks. Especially since Connor blames me. The whole mess was the crewmen's fault."

Revel looked past her with a thousand-yard stare. Maybe he was reliving the firefight. No matter how she felt, it must be worse for a person who'd never seen a gun to encounter two men shooting wildly in the night. Revel's unblinking eyes turned back to her, but he didn't speak.

Unable to interpret the look on his face, she busied herself at the sink by filling the water bottle for her backpack. "I'd understand if you blame me too."

"No." His brow furrowed and he frowned like he was pained by what she suggested. "No, I don't blame you for what happened."

A reply of thanks dissolved on her tongue. Even if he didn't blame her, the urge to apologize kept her from leaving the kitchen.

The kettle on the stove whistled, diverting their attention. He slowly moved away, leaving hope in the air.

It was nice to know the man who apprehended her two days ago now sympathized with her.

He poured boiling water over a strainer full of dark green leaves. "Would you like a cup of coffee?"

The scent of her favorite morning beverage filled the room, but whatever he was making wasn't coffee. She hooked her thumbs in her backpack straps. "No, I should go. Like I said, I have to do the next thing."

"And find Tim?"

When she nodded, he set the kettle on an iron trivet and walked toward the back door. "I'm coming too."

"You don't have to."

"Yes, I do," he said, taking a jacket from a row of silver hooks in the wall by the door.

When she'd dreamed of the life she might live in the Land, she hadn't considered the traditionalist culture meant having men hover over her as if she couldn't protect herself. They had no idea what she was capable of. "Look, Revel, I can take care of myself."

Though her words came out with more of a defensive tone than she'd intended, Revel simply nodded. "I know you don't need me to go with you, but I need to do the next thing too." He reached around her and opened the door. "The reason I'm up early is to go back to the shore. It bothered me that we didn't find your friend yesterday. The way I see it, you are welcome to go with me." A slight grin curved the edge of his mouth. "After you, ma'am."

Ma'am? She would let that one slide. If his manners were supposed to mean anything more than kindness, he was in for disappointment. Her desire for finding a family in no way included making one. She didn't return his grin. "Fine. We can split up and cover more ground. *Two is better than one—*"

"Because they have a good reward for their labor."

His continuance of the Bible verse she'd started to recite made her smile. "Yeah, something like that."

He closed the door behind them. "How is your leg?"

"Hm? Oh, fine." She inhaled the humid predawn air and glanced at Revel's profile. "It's scarred, but the gray leaf medicine healed the wound quickly. It was amazing."

"That's what I've heard."

"You never needed it?"

He shook his head. "But the gray leaf medicine saved my brother James's life a couple of months ago. He hated it."

Recalling the euphoric sensation, she wondered how the inhabitants of the Land resisted drinking cup after cup of it simply to feel good. "Your brother hated drinking the gray leaf tea?"

"Many people don't like it."

She walked between the back of the house and the doctor's office. The downstairs windows were dark, but the glow of a lantern illumined an upstairs window. Sophia must be up early. She looked back at Revel. "Why would someone not like the gray leaf?"

"Probably fear."

"Of what?"

"Old stories. There's one about how a horse died after it ate a few gray leaves. One about how the gray leaf tea put a young woman in a coma and she almost died. Another says it made a man infertile. Those sorts of stories."

"So, is the gray leaf unreliable or is the folklore?"

"Probably both." Revel chuckled. There was more to him than shell-shocked regret. He motioned to the ground as they navigated between trees. "Watch your step through here. Lots of roots."

Twigs crackled with each footstep when they neared the forest at the back of John's property. The oval-shaped moon wasn't as bright as it had been two nights ago, and first light had yet to grace the sky. She didn't need much light to know her way to the shore by now. She'd walked this path several times already, having spent yesterday combing the shore and only returning to the house when John told her it was mealtime.

The hum of the waves reminded Bailey of the beaches in Accomack, especially after the barrier islands had washed away. As they walked toward the waterline on the hard-packed sand, the black sky lightened to gray then to pale lavender.

Revel put a hand in front of her, stopping her. "Don't go any closer to the water. The tide is about to change. The surface is only calm for a few minutes during the full moon—like it was when you came ashore night before last."

At first, she found his warning overcautious, but the growing light gave her a clearer look at the incoming water. Quick swirls in the sand under the receding waves demonstrated its harsh undertow. She didn't need to go into the water anyway. Tim was on the shore somewhere; she just knew it. She scanned the beach in both directions. "Where to start?"

Revel pointed south. "Since we won't be able to go past the bluffs once the tide comes in, let's start there."

She hadn't meant to ask for his advice but took it anyway. "That's what I was thinking."

Seagulls scurried up and down the shore. The light of the coming dawn grew, aiding her search for any sign of Professor Tim. It had been thirty-six hours since they'd said goodbye on the yacht. Her last image of him was while he was packing his bag, wearing the white bucket hat he claimed was lucky. The hat didn't matter as much as what he'd put in his bag. "I hope he has his medicine with him."

"What type of medicine?"

"Insulin. He's diabetic."

Revel took his eyes off the beach long enough to look at her. "What would happen to him if he didn't have it?"

"Sometimes he can go awhile without it and feel fine. But if his blood sugar dropped low enough, he could get very sick." She had to shout over the waves' loud crashing. "I didn't bring him out here to die. I'm counting on Tim's survival to make all of this okay."

"What do you mean?"

"If he dies, it is all my fault."

Revel stopped walking. Bailey had said too much. She hadn't meant to create a sentimental moment with him. Something about his openness made her let down her guard. She shouldn't. Ever.

But he wasn't looking at her; he was looking past her at some tussock grass where the wind-tossed sand met the wilderness. Something yellow was caught in the bottom of the grass.

"What's that?" he asked, pointing to it.

She hurried ahead of him to check it out. Waist-high grass blades swished in the breeze. She pushed the long blades out of her face and grabbed the wet object. The emblem on it matched the yacht company's logo. "It's a life vest."

At her announcement, Revel's eyes widened. He jumped toward the high grass and searched frantically. Bailey dropped the vest and moved the surrounding grass, folding it in one direction then the other. "Tim? Tim?"

Her calls went unanswered.

After several minutes of searching, Revel had gone some twenty yards down the shore. His tall frame was bent over, swallowed by high grass. He stood erect and cupped his hands around his mouth. "Bailey! Come here!"

The ocean's furious waves crashed against the rocks between the sea and the tall grass, spraying her with salty mist. She ran toward Revel. He knelt to the ground and stood again, holding up something white. It was made of thick cloth and regained its shape when he gave it a quick shake. Part of it was embroidered with a little black giraffe silhouette.

Bailey's feet slowed as she got closer. Each step felt like she was walking in thick tar. "That is Tim's lucky hat."

She took the hat from Revel. Tim never would have removed his lucky hat. A scientist with a superstition. Even he'd laughed at himself for that one. Everything else that had been in his boat, including his remains, would soon wash ashore if it hadn't already. She rubbed a thumb over the embroidered giraffe. "He didn't survive, did—" her voice caught, taking her words and her hope with it.

Revel shook his head. "I'm so sorry, Bailey."

CHAPTER FIFTEEN

An overcast sky dimmed the afternoon light in the kitchen, so Eva opened the pantry doors wider to see inside it. She turned the jars on the shelves to check their labels, and Sybil immediately straightened the jars back into perfect rows. After making a note on her inventory list, Eva chuckled at Sybil. "Could you at least wait until I have my arms out of the way before you start that?"

"Start what?" Sybil frowned, drawing her full lips into a cute pout.

"You know exactly what."

"You get to have your messy office, and I get to keep my kitchen tidy."

"Fair enough."

Sybil's expression swiftly changed then as though she suddenly had a secret. "Did he say anything before he left this morning?"

"Who?"

A faint blush colored Sybil's cheeks. "Isaac."

"Isaac Owens? About the farm job?"

"Yes, did he accept your offer?"

Eva counted the cans of cherries next. "He did." Just as she wrote down the number, Sybil squealed like a wrong note on the violin. The sound startled Eva, and she broke the tip of her pencil. "What was that for?"

Sybil's smile broadened. "When does he start?"

The pure bliss in her sister's eyes betrayed her infatuation. Still, Eva had to ask. "Are you intrigued with him?"

"No." She tried to erase the emotion from her face to no avail. "No, I'm just thrilled we will finally have more help around here. For Leonard and Father and you, of course. I know how badly you wanted to hire someone." She pretended to busy herself with the jars, but another happy squeal filled the pantry.

Eva set her pencil and notebook on a shelf and turned her sister by the shoulders. "Tell me everything."

Sybil's blue eyes were brighter than ever. "He came into the kitchen after dinner last night and said my cooking was delicious."

"And?"

"And I told him thank you. At least I think that's what I said."

"And?"

"And then he said goodnight."

There had to be more interaction between them to make Sybil fall in love. Eva waved a hand prompting her sister to continue. "And?"

"And…" Sybil shrugged. "He was so handsome, and the way he said it was so sincere. He looked at me like I was more than a cook. Like I mattered. Isn't he wonderful?"

"That was it? He complimented your cooking and you fell in love. Don't be so quick to give your heart away, Syb."

"I'm not giving anything away. It was sweet, that's all." Her gaze drifted to the ceiling. "There was something about him that was just so... so..."

"Handsome? Yes, I know."

"When does he move here?"

"He has to work at his current job until his boss finds someone to replace him."

"Will he still come to stay at the inn while trading until he can work here forever?"

Eva had never seen her sister in love before. She half wanted to squeal along with her and half wanted to send a message to Isaac, revoking the job offer. What if he didn't share Sybil's feelings? What if he moved here to do a job and broke her sister's heart? There was only one way to deal with this: get back to work. She picked up her pencil and pointed into the pantry. "It will probably be a couple of months before he moves here. I'd like to finish taking inventory before then, all right?"

As Sybil smiled in response, the screen door slammed and Zeke ran into the kitchen, waving his hands. "Mama! Mama, come quick!"

He'd probably found a dead bird or his puppy had pulled the laundry off the line. Eva sighed at her adorably flustered son and slid her pencil into her apron pocket. "What is it, Zeke?"

Zeke's red face huffed with each quick breath. He shook his head frantically. "It's Leonard. He fell from the harvester, and Solo had to carry him to the cottage."

Sybil sucked in a shocked breath.

The terror in Zeke's eyes held more than childish exaggeration. Eva's heart doubled its pace. She pointed at the staircase. "Go tell Claudia what happened. She's upstairs, changing sheets." Then she looked at Sybil. "Make some gray leaf tea in case Leonard is injured."

As Zeke ran down the hallway and Sybil turned to the stove, Eva hurried out the side door toward the cottage. The screen banged behind her, and her skirt swished with each fearful stride.

She found Leonard inside the cozy cottage's only bedroom. He was lying on top of the quilted bed, unresponsive. Solo was gently pulling the older man's boots off his feet. He snapped his concerned face toward the bedroom doorway when Eva stepped in.

"What happened?" she demanded, as she rushed to Leonard's side.

"I'm not sure. I think he slipped coming down from the harvester. He hit the ground hard." A catch broke Solo's voice. "I got to him as quick as I could."

She lifted Leonard's limp hand, wondering where exactly doctors touched to feel a heartbeat. Leonard's chest rose and fell steadily, so he was still breathing. Her own pulse thudded in her ears. She tried to speak with a calm voice as if she were just waking him from a nap. "Leonard? Leonard, it's Eva. Can you hear me?"

Solo was motionless, hovering over Leonard from the other side of the bed, waiting for a response too.

None came.

The cottage door opened, and Claudia dashed inside with Zeke close behind her. Solo stepped away from the bed as the room got crowded.

Claudia touched her husband's face with desperate hands. "Oh, Leonard! Speak to me!"

Solo set Leonard's boots on the floor at the foot of the bed and backed out of the room. "I can ride to Riverside to get the doctor, if you think I should."

Tears slid down Claudia's face. Her hands shook. "Leonard, please open your eyes."

Eva's heart ached for Claudia. She knew what it felt like to beg a husband to wake up. Hers never did. A lump of emotion clogged her throat. She gave Leonard's hand one last rub and stood. "We will get the doctor here as quickly as we can, and Sybil is making gray leaf tea."

Zeke flung his arms around her waist, weeping.

She stroked his hair gently while she spoke to Solo. "Yes, please get the doctor. You won't make it to Riverside until after dark. You will have to pace the horse, so you don't wear him out before you get there."

He squared his shoulders. "I know how to handle a horse."

She hadn't meant to offend the one man she needed. "Yes, of course you do." She touched his arm. "I'll pack food for you and for the doctor to eat on the ride back here tomorrow. Ask father which of our horses would be best to take."

Solo slapped on his hat then flashed his confident gaze at her over his shoulder. "I already know."

CHAPTER SIXTEEN

Eva shifted a lunch basket to the crook of her arm then knocked softly on the cottage door. When no one answered, she let herself in. The iron hinges on the door creaked mournfully as she closed it behind her.

Claudia was sitting in a cane-back rocking chair beside the bed where Leonard had been lying unconscious since yesterday afternoon. When the older woman glanced up, Eva raised the basket. "I brought you lunch."

"Not hungry."

"You should eat. He will need you to be strong when he wakes up." Though the words were different, the bolstered hope in her tone reminded her of the way people spoke to her after Ezekiel's death. That was different. Her husband had died in his sleep; Leonard was still breathing. And they didn't know what injury Leonard had sustained in the fall—there were no bruises or cuts. He might awaken at any moment and be fine.

She would not lose hope, nor would she forget how it felt to lose her husband. She set the food basket on a side table and knelt by Claudia. "Any change?"

Claudia shook her head. "Every hour or so he groans and shifts a little. That's it." Her chin quivered and she sniffed. "He won't open his eyes. Won't say anything to me. I asked him to squeeze my hand if he could hear me, but he didn't respond."

"I'm so sorry." She rubbed Claudia's arm the same way Claudia had rubbed hers when Ezekiel was buried. "At least he is stirring every so often. That's a good sign."

Claudia looked up with rounded eyes as if she was eager to believe anything hopeful. "Do you think so?"

"Yes, I do. We'll keep praying for him and trust the Lord to heal him."

Hoofbeats thudded the ground outside the cottage. Eva stood and peeled the curtain away from the window. "They're here!"

As she opened the door, Solo swung down from a white horse Eva didn't recognize. He must have swapped her father's horse in Riverside for a fresh horse. He looped the reins around a hitching post, and the doctor did the same. Both men walked stiffly toward the cottage, backs bent from riding for several hours straight.

Solo stopped before the door and let the doctor enter first. He took off his hat. "Eva, this is Doc—"

"We've met." She hadn't seen the man since Ezekiel's death. "Thank you for coming, Doctor."

The gray-haired gentleman nodded once.

Eva opened her hand toward the bedroom door. "Through there."

She stayed in the cottage's tight entryway with Solo while the doctor went into the bedroom and closed the door. Claudia's muffled voice explained Leonard's condition and the doctor asked her questions. It was an exchange Eva had encountered before and hoped never to again.

She faced the open doorway and scanned the back of the inn across the yard. Sybil stepped out to the side porch and rang the lunch bell. Eva's vision lost focus as she watched her sister. "I told Zeke to eat lunch with his grandpa, but he's probably too worried to eat."

Solo caught her eye. "I can stay with the doc if you need to go back to the house."

"No, I want to be here for Claudia in case it's bad news."

The concern in Solo's unrelenting gaze made her want to talk to him, to tell him everything, but she couldn't. Not everything, not now. She returned her stare to the back of the inn. "Zeke was pretty upset this morning at breakfast. He has eaten every meal at the same table with Father and Leonard and Claudia his whole life. He doesn't understand why Leonard won't wake up. I should go check on him."

Solo put a warm hand on her shoulder. "Go ahead. I'll stay here with them."

The faint sound of Claudia's sniffles came from the bedroom. Eva's insides ached. "No, I shouldn't leave now."

Dark circles under his eyes attested to his lack of sleep last night. He pointed a thumb toward the inn. "Would you like me to go check on Zeke?"

"You don't have to. You've already done so much. Thank you for getting the doctor. I don't know what we would have done without you."

He didn't respond but only studied her. It was as if he had something to say but wouldn't. It was probably her imagination; she hadn't slept much last night either.

Finally, he nodded. "I'll go check on Zeke and then take the horses to the barn. The doc will need to stay here tonight. Maybe tomorrow depending on Leonard's condition."

"Yes, of course. We have an open guest room."

He lifted his strong chin at the white horse that was munching on the grass around the hitching post. "I had to leave your father's horse in Riverside. He was worn out. I made a swap at the ranch where I work."

The same thing had happened when a trader had raced to get the doctor for Ezekiel. A wave of emotion lightened her head. She leaned a hand against the wall. "Right, well. I'm sure that will all get worked out. If Zeke needs me—"

"I'll come and get you." He put his hat back on. "Did anyone do Leonard's chores today?"

"One of the traders stayed a couple of hours and helped out, but Father wasn't able to do his work in the stable."

"I'll pitch in after lunch."

"You don't have to."

He stepped out to the porch then stopped and looked back at her. "Yes, Eva, I do."

She watched him walk toward the house, his gait strong and sure even though he'd been riding for hours. The reason he had come to stay at the inn and the deal he'd made with her father no longer mattered. He was here now and they needed him. She needed him.

"Mrs. Vestal?" the doctor said from the bedroom doorway.

She held her breath. "Will Leonard be all right?"

The doctor waved her into the bedroom, so she stood beside Claudia, who was wiping her eyes with an embroidered handkerchief. He glanced between them and kept his kind voice low. "Leonard isn't unconscious because of the fall yesterday. He fell because he lost consciousness. I believe he had a stroke."

Claudia choked on a sob. Eva put her arm around Claudia's shoulders but kept her attention on the doctor so he would continue his assessment. "Will he recover?"

The answer was clear in the brief downcast of the doctor's gaze. She'd seen that look before. He pressed his lips together. "The fact that he has stirred a few times and tried to speak gives me hope, but most patients don't fully recover all their faculties after such an episode."

"Would gray leaf tea help him?"

"It might. If he awakens enough to swallow, that should be the first drink he is given."

As the doctor closed his medical bag and stepped out of the room, Claudia's quiet weeping erupted into wails of agony. Eva held her and cried too.

CHAPTER SEVENTEEN

For two weeks Bailey isolated herself in the borrowed bedroom in John Colburn's home, needing solitude to process everything that had happened. She'd gone from forging a living as a bartender in Virginia while waiting for a plant research job, to being dragged into Justin Mercer's impossible tale of a miracle plant from a hidden land, to finding herself in that land, and now mourning the loss of the only person who truly knew her.

Regaining focus after a tragedy usually didn't take her long. That was how she'd survived life so far. But even after two weeks of mourning, her mind was reluctant to move on. It was as though she was stuck in the moment of seeing the evidence of Tim's death.

They both had accepted the risks in coming here. She'd wondered if her life would end during their attempt to find the Land, or if they might all die at sea, but she never thought she alone would survive the journey. Just like she was the only surviving member of her biological family, her martial arts team, her college class.

This time, her survival was different. After the other sudden life changes she'd experienced, there was always one person from her past who went with her into the next phase. She changed schools nine times during junior high and high school but had the same martial arts coach. Then in college when the water poisoning and war canceled classes and killed her friends, Professor Tim was still there for her.

But not any longer.

Every relationship from her former life was gone now. She was alone. Not long ago she'd told Revel she was a survivor, like it was a good thing. It didn't feel so good anymore. Not when she was this alone.

Coach used to say Bailey was a survivor because of her mental outlook. She saw threats as challenges and disasters as opportunities. She needed to find the strength to pick herself up and carry on this time.

Each day since losing Tim, she'd only left the bedroom to go to the bathroom and when John summoned her to the kitchen for a meal. Everyone in the Colburn house respectfully left her to her mourning as she'd asked, but the concern in their eyes was growing, especially in Revel's. But sometimes, the way he looked away from her more than at her exuded guilt rather than pity. The firefight was the crewmen's fault and John said the churning waves were to blame for Tim's loss. Revel had no reason to feel guilty, but Bailey didn't have the capacity to think about someone else's problems right now.

Today felt just like yesterday. The morning bled into afternoon like an open wound. Now the big house was quiet. John was at his office at the church. Connor and Revel were out doing farm chores or whatever it was that made them smell like manure and sweat when they came inside late in the afternoons. Lydia and Sophia were working in the medical cottage. Occasionally, one of the women would come back into the house with the baby. Their kitchen noise would travel down the hallway for a few minutes, then all would go quiet again.

Bailey stood from the rocking chair where she'd watched the gray leaf tree shadows stretch across the back lawn. She couldn't sit in isolation any longer. This wasn't like her. Only she could put an end to it.

Out in the living room, the baby babbled and Sophia's soft voice followed. Lydia must be in the cottage with a patient if Sophia was babysitting Andrew in the house.

The only voice Bailey wanted to hear was Professor Tim's. She walked to the lacquered wardrobe on the far side of the dark room and opened its smooth doors. Her backpack at the bottom of the wardrobe was still packed. She dug out the two-way radio then crouched by the open wardrobe and pressed the power switch.

Nothing but static.

Why was she tormenting herself like this? Tim hadn't survived. They had combed the beach and found a dozen items from his boat, including his eyeglasses and a cracked oar. What more proof did she need? He was gone, his body dragged out to sea by the currents. She must accept it.

Getting her wrist broken in a tournament in ninth grade hadn't made her cry. Having to leave the rural farmhouse where she'd spent one blissful summer in the garden with Mrs. Polk didn't bring her to tears. Being forced to opt into the sterilization program to qualify for a college grant hadn't broken her spirit. Yet, here she was wallowing when the man she grieved for would have told her to cry it out, wipe her eyes, and get back to work.

Logic was her best defense. Tim had taught her that. The sooner she acknowledged the truth of her circumstances, the sooner she could make a life in the Land.

She should use her research knowledge to classify the gray leaf tree. Lydia and Sophia spent half their time out in the medical cottage looking for new ways to use the medicinal plant. She could be out there with them, sharing her expertise and helping to make a difference in the lives of good people, but instead she was trapping herself in a quiet Victorian-era bedroom. Not exactly the behavior of a self-proclaimed survivor.

The next thing. She had to do the next thing. The only choice more repugnant than giving up was giving in to self-pity. Her bulging backpack caught her eye. Refusing to be oppressed by emotion for one more moment, she turned off the radio and started to unpack.

The purpose of coming to the Land was to start a new life. The outside world was dead to her with its wars and plagues and terrorism. Here in the Land she could connect with her long-lost relatives, make new friends, and study plants—or better yet—plant a garden. She could explore the Land in peace. This was a new opportunity, and every positive voice from her past told her to take hold of it with all her strength.

Where had her strength gone? It was like Professor Tim's death had knocked the wind out of her spirit. She closed her eyes briefly. "God give me strength."

She opened her eyes and laid her spare t-shirt and socks inside one of the wardrobe's drawers then nestled her New Testament between them. Everything else she had was survival gear. She opened a second drawer and dumped the contents of her backpack into it. It seemed silly to carry around a compact thermal blanket when she'd been given a warm, clean bed to sleep in. And what good were stormproof matches when John Colburn's house had wood-burning fireplaces?

She'd come to the Land prepared but for all the wrong scenarios. Reality wrestled for freedom in her head. She no longer needed to focus on surviving, no matter how much her mind wanted to remain in survival mode. The truth was: she was alone in the Land but safe, mourning an end but being offered a new beginning, completing an adventure but embarking on an uncharted journey.

Outside the window, a soft breeze stirred the branches of two willow trees, their leaves dulled by autumn's caress. The pretty landscape called to her. She hadn't checked out the garden plants yet. She'd only been from the kitchen door to the cottage to the shore.

There was more to this land, to this village, even to John Colburn's property, and it was time she explored. She'd traveled all this way to find the family she'd never had in the peaceful land she'd always dreamed of. The least she could do was leave the bedroom.

She tucked her empty backpack into the bottom of the wardrobe and stood. As soon as she closed the cabinet, a light knock vibrated the bedroom door.

"Come in."

Sophia opened the door a few inches and poked her head into the room. Lydia's son was on her hip. His curious brown eyes were trying to peek in.

Bailey walked to the door and pulled it open all the way. "What's up?"

Sophia held out a bundle of light blue cloth. "The seamstress delivered these for you. Lydia asked her to make you two new day dresses. Mrs. McIntosh—she makes all our clothes—will come back tomorrow to do your alterations. I asked her to wait until next week because we are giving you time to yourself, but she said you will need more clothes sooner than that."

"Thanks." Bailey accepted the cloth and unfolded the dresses, which were two different designs but were made of the same soft, blue fabric. She held a dress in each hand. One had a ribbed bodice attached to a full skirt, while the other was one piece with pearl buttons down the front. Both had long sleeves, and neither was like anything she would ever wear. "They're really... ladylike."

Sophia smiled and stepped farther into the room, taking Bailey's comment as a compliment. She wore a plum-colored design similar to the full-skirted dress Bailey was holding in her left hand. Sophia rubbed the fabric between her thumb and forefinger. "Mrs. McIntosh uses a heavy cotton, so it should last a long time."

Bailey had never thought much about the fabric of her clothes. When she'd shopped for clothes before the war, *washable* had been her only concern. She rubbed the material of the pilgrim-esque dress the way Sophia had. "How practical."

"Dr. Bradshaw said this color was the closest Mrs. McIntosh had to your favorite trousers."

"My what?"

"The blue trousers you always wear."

"My jeans?"

Sophia adjusted the baby on her hip. "Yes, Dr. Bradshaw thought you might feel more comfortable here if she had clothes made for you in a color you already wear."

"That's really… sweet." It wasn't the color that made a difference in her comfort but the type of clothes. She hadn't worn a dress since kindergarten and that was only because her foster mom at the time took her to a thrift store on Dollar-Per-Bag Day and stuffed a plastic grocery sack full of little dresses. Some had been two sizes too big; some were faded. One had a splotch of melted crayon stuck to the hem. The dresses made her run slowly and play awkwardly. She'd never worn a dress again.

Bailey laid the dresses on the foot of the bed. "Can your seamstress make pants?"

"For whom?"

"Me."

Sophia crinkled her petite nose. "Why would you want more trousers?"

"That's what I wear."

"All the time?" Sophia looked at the wardrobe as if the answer were hiding behind its doors. "Like a man?"

"No, not *like a man*. Women wear pants."

"Plain women."

"So maybe I'm plain."

Sophia tilted her head and her pretty brow furrowed. "Oh, don't say that."

"I wasn't criticizing myself. I—"

"You're not at all plain. You're an attractive woman. You will meet a man one day, I'm sure of it."

A laugh bubbled out of Bailey's throat. "I'm not looking to attract a man. Believe me. But thanks for that. It feels good to laugh."

A reluctant smile dimpled Sophia's rosy cheeks. "Mrs. McIntosh docs excellent tailoring, so I'm sure you will be just as comfortable in these dresses as you are in trousers."

Bailey doubted that. "I'll stick to my jeans, thanks." She stepped into her hiking shoes and bent to tie the laces. "I like to keep moving and not have to worry about flowy skirts. Besides, you can't surprise a handsy guy with a roundhouse kick to the jaw when you have eight yards of fabric holding your leg down."

Sophia's eyes bulged.

"I was just kidding."

"Oh."

Bailey offered a mischievous grin. "Unless he deserves it."

Sophia's horrified expression eased, and she giggled. "I suppose you're right."

"Of course, I'm right." Bailey double knotted her shoelaces and stood. "Thanks for bringing the clothes to me. I have to go."

Sophia stepped to the side and let Bailey pass. "I'm glad you're feeling better."

"Yeah, me too."

"Would you like to try on your dresses?"

"Could I do it later? I was just on my way out."

"Of course."

Bailey hurried out of the house before Sophia could say anything else about clothes. It wasn't that she didn't like the girl. Fitting into an old-school society wasn't going to be as simple as putting on a dress. To Sophia—and probably the rest of the women here in the Land—the dress symbolized their sacred femininity, which was fine for them. But to Bailey, wearing a dress meant slowing down, being less prepared to defend herself, depending on a man for things she could do herself. She'd have a talk with the seamstress soon and get some pants made. But for today, she needed to go explore.

As she stepped out the kitchen doorway, John was walking up the drive, holding several books in the bend of his arm. "Good to see you out-of-doors, Bailey. There is something I would like to ask you."

She stopped in the house's long shadow. "What's up?"

A fatherly grin reached his eyes. "That is one of Connor's expressions. It is delightful to hear it in a female voice."

Any comparison to a military man rankled. "I hate to break it to you, but I'm not a female version of Connor."

His grin receded. "I meant no offense."

"I'm not offended." Even as the words came out of her mouth, she crossed her arms. "Connor and I have nothing in common other than the fact we were both born in America and we both ended up in the Land."

John switched the books to his other arm. "And you both came into my household with hearts full of pain."

"Yeah, so? The outside world is dangerous. Life is dangerous." She remembered what a social worker said when her mom died in prison. "Life is full of loss."

"It is also full of blessing." John captured her attention with his intense gaze. "But we close ourselves off to the blessings when we refuse to acknowledge the loss."

A kid didn't endure the upbringing Bailey had without hearing this kind of speech from the occasional well-meaning grown-up. They were usually trying to make themselves feel better about her circumstances. "I know, I know."

"Do you?" John angled his chin and asked more with his eyes than with his words.

Professor Tim used to respond the same way when she flippantly used that phrase. Both men had that dad-to-everyone thing going on. And they were both right.

She shrugged off the default childish attitude that always reared up when history repeated itself. "Sorry. It's just that I've had so much loss, I wouldn't know which one to acknowledge first."

"Start with what happened recently. Two weeks ago, you lost a man who meant a great deal to you. Since his remains were never found, there was no burial. Perhaps a memorial service would give you the closure you need. That is what I wanted to ask you about. It is our tradition in the Land to acknowledge every death and pay respect, but since the men who died coming here did so under… unique circumstances, we have kept the situation private. The village of Good Springs is filled with compassionate people who are now your neighbors. If I told the church what happened, they would be pleased to help you with your loss."

She was ready to remove her focus from Tim's death. The shock had passed. All that remained was the heavy grief that always lurked under the surface of her fractured heart. Crying in front of strangers wouldn't help that. She scanned the parts of the property she was anxious to explore. "Thanks, but I'd rather not make a big deal out of it. If only the people involved know about what happened when I arrived, I'd like to keep it that way."

John scratched his trimmed gray beard. "What about a private ceremony with just my household?"

"Since none of you knew Tim, it would be kind of pointless."

"It would give you a chance to tell us about him and what he meant to you."

There was no way she would put herself in the center of that kind of attention, especially with people she barely knew. "No. I'm fine, really. I have my own way of dealing with things."

John nodded as if in agreement, but unease still marked his expression. "Very well." He gave her shoulder a fatherly pat then walked into the kitchen.

She followed the row of azaleas and hydrangeas around the back of the house. The shrubs' leaves were firm and fungus free. Two willow trees stood in the middle of the back yard. They were the same trees she'd watched from her bedroom window for the past two weeks.

She ambled between the willows and turned to face the house. The bedroom she was staying in was on the bottom floor on the north end. The high narrow window in the center of the bottom floor allowed light and air into the bathroom. So, the window on the south end of the house must be the guest room where Revel was staying.

John had introduced Revel as his *houseguest*. Every morning after breakfast, Revel left with Connor to do chores. There might be work she could do here on the property to earn her keep too. The landscaping was well cared for, but maybe they had a vegetable garden that needed tending.

A pleasant breeze blew in from the nearby ocean, mixing the scents of salt and sea with the pine and gray leaf trees. She inhaled deeply, welcoming the satiating aromas. It would be easy to enjoy her time here. If only she could allow herself to build a life in this new place, if not for herself, for Tim, for Coach, or for the lost little girl she once was who yearned for a safe and quiet life in the country.

Yes, for them she would push beyond survival. She'd never had the chance before. Maybe that was why God had spared her. Maybe this was her chance to find out what she was created for.

CHAPTER EIGHTEEN

Not long after dinner, the inn quieted down for the night. The guests went to their rooms or the bunkhouse earlier than they used to. Before Leonard's stroke, Frederick had always kept them entertained after dinner, and the lively conversations would roll until the tired travelers were ready for bed. But tonight, Frederick had stayed quiet at dinner, staring solemnly at the two empty seats at his table, like he had at every meal for the past three weeks.

Solo missed the games of cards that used to start after dessert and how Eva and Sybil would join in once their hosting chores were done. He missed how Zeke would get sleepy and sit in Claudia's lap until his mama came out of the kitchen. Lately, Claudia ate her meals in the cottage at Leonard's side, and Zeke sat by his grandfather in silence.

The inn wasn't the same with the family's current woes. Solo understood their need for rest and quiet. Since taking on Leonard's farm chores and some of the stable work, by evening he was too tired to write. But tonight, he wasn't ready to go up to his room just yet.

He wandered out the front door and sat in the swing on the east side of the long porch. From there, he had a solemn view of last light's fading glow in the western sky. With his room situated on the back side of the house, he rarely got to see this aspect at night.

The swing's rusty chain buzzed rhythmically when he set the bench seat in motion. The curtains on the inside of the window adjacent the swing were parted, and a lamp in Eva's office illuminated her disorganized desk. She must be planning to work in there after Zeke fell asleep upstairs. How she kept this place running while raising a son and doing half of Claudia's chores was astonishing!

He returned his gaze to the sky, but the last slip of soft light disappeared. Only darkness pitted with emerging starlight remained. He should go up to his room and write, but the cool air and gently squeaking swing lulled him to stay put.

This was the twenty-third of his forty-night stay at the inn. Only seventeen left. He'd barely written one children's story. Nothing was going like he'd planned, but he couldn't feel sorry for himself. After all, Leonard and Claudia were having a much harder time than he was.

The front door opened and Zeke's growing puppy ran out ahead of Eva. She closed the door behind her and pulled a long pin out of her hair. Her tresses fell in a velvety cascade down her back. The swing's creak got her attention. "I didn't know anyone was out here." She pointed at the puppy. "I had to bring Joshua out before bedtime."

Solo suddenly wanted her company more than he wanted to be alone. "Don't mind me. I'm just enjoying the cool air."

She wrapped her arms under her woolen shawl. "It is a bit chilly out here." She led the puppy to the grass beyond a line of evergreen shrubs then spoke to Solo over the porch railing. "Thanks for doing the milking this morning and for working in the stables again today."

"You're welcome."

"When I took dinner to the cottage tonight, Leonard said he's grateful for all that you are doing." Her gaze lowered to the ground. "At least, I think that was what he said."

Solo was less concerned with getting their appreciation as he was taking away some of her burden. "Don't worry. Leonard's speech will clear up in no time."

Eva blew out a long breath through pursed lips. "I hope so."

"A week ago, we didn't expect him ever to talk again, so this is progress. Remember what the doctor said."

She lifted a hand. "I know. And I'm trying to stay positive, especially in front of Leonard and Claudia."

Joshua finished his business and scrambled up the porch, his claws clinking on the painted wooden steps. The puppy zipped past Eva and ran straight to Solo. He scooped the dog up. "You've grown like a weed since I brought you here."

Eva rounded the column and walked toward the swing but didn't sit. "Zeke feeds him from the table."

The dog plopped down on the swing beside Solo. He petted the puppy while he started swinging again. "I used to sneak table scraps to my dog when I was a boy. My mother would swat my hand if she caught me."

That brought a grin to Eva's full lips. After a moment her grin slowly dissolved. "I wouldn't swat Zeke. It drives me mad when people hit children." She turned her face toward the office window beside them. "I should finish my paperwork, but I don't want to go back inside."

"Then don't." He lifted the puppy and scooted over to make room for her on the swing.

She glanced at the seat then him and finally shrugged. "Why not?"

A twinge of victory bolstered his confidence. The swing wriggled beneath him as she got settled. Then he set it in motion again, slowly rocking up and back. The wind stirred the scent of Eva's soap and skin, mesmerizing him. As he breathed it in, his shoulders relaxed and his heart pumped renewed blood through his system.

A desire to give her anything and everything she could ever want woke him from his evening doldrums. He watched her in his peripheral vision, not wanting to stare at her and scare her away.

What did she want that he could give her? She needed help with the farm chores, but he was already doing all he could. She needed help watching Zeke while keeping an eye out for her aging father and managing the temporary workers, but he did that too. She hadn't asked anything else of him... except on that first night he was in his room and she came to the door.

What if he gave in to her demand from that night and told her why he'd come to the inn? Would it build her trust in him or reignite her suspicion? She shifted on the swing, and her arm brushed his. His stomach knotted like the first time he'd wanted to kiss a girl in the schoolyard.

That was different... juvenile. Now he was a grown man and the feelings swirling inside him weren't curiosity or simply physical attraction. This was so much more. Eva was a powerful woman he could love *and* respect.

His granddad had always said every good relationship was built on honesty. If he wanted to get to know her, he had to let her know him. He took one more deep inhale of her scent and wiped his sweaty palm on his trousers. "I came to the inn to write… to write a book of children's stories."

She turned her chin toward him but kept her gaze straight ahead. "Children's stories?"

"My granddad was a storyteller and made up the best stories, fables mostly. I have a few of my own. I always wanted to write them down and have it turned into a children's book."

She didn't say anything, so he kept talking.

"Your father knew my granddad from way back. One day a couple of years ago, he asked me if I remembered any of my granddad's stories. I told him I did and I had come up with my own too. He encouraged me to get them on paper. I tried." He stole a quick glance to see if her expression gave away her opinion. It didn't, so he kept talking. "There isn't any privacy in the bunkhouse at the ranch in Riverside, and I still had awhile to work before I got my own land. Your father invited me here for a few weeks, but I couldn't take a room for nothing, so I stored up credit with him over the past two years."

Eva released a defeated breath and hung her head. "I'm so sorry for accusing you of—"

He hadn't meant to shame her. "Please don't. That's not why I'm telling you."

Her voice lacked its usual fullness. "Then why are you telling me this now?"

Something told him to back down, that this wasn't the time, that he wasn't man enough for a strong woman like Eva. He was just a horse breeder from someone else's ranch, not even second in command. His fingers stilled their petting as the puppy lying against him fell asleep.

Eva needed a man who matched her force outwardly as much as inwardly, a man whose presence made other men cower. He wasn't that man; he had his defects.

He also had a faithful heart filled with the desire to love this woman and her son, to keep them safe, to make them his family. He stopped the swing with his feet. "I want you to know the truth."

She raised her head. "The truth?"

He caught her eye, needing her to see his sincerity. "I want you to know you can trust me."

She lowered her chin. "Solo, if there is one person I've come to count on in the past few weeks, it's you. With my inn, with my son. I wouldn't let Zeke follow you around all day if I didn't trust you."

That was all he needed for now but not all he wanted. He faced the dark horizon and put his arm over the back of the swing behind her then waited for her reaction. She didn't lean in, nor did she pull away.

Just as he turned his face to tell her he was glad he'd come to the inn even if things weren't going how he'd planned, she looked up at him. They both froze, their lips inches apart. Her eyelashes fluttered as she gazed at his mouth. Everything inside him yearned to kiss her, and from her staggered breath, he guessed she would let him.

If he did kiss her, she might think that was why he'd opened up to her, that he was only building her trust so he could take more from her. It wasn't the reason at all, and he certainly wasn't going to risk losing her trust now. He broke their gaze and turned his face away, focusing on no particular point in the dark as he set the swing in motion again.

CHAPTER NINETEEN

Eva carried a stack of dirty plates to the kitchen after lunch and knocked the leftover fragments of Sybil's delicious baked trout into the scrap pan for the chickens. Most of last night's guests had left this morning, save for a family from Pleasant Valley and two traders who'd stayed to help with the farming. With no new arrivals scheduled for tonight, Eva expected the inn to be quiet.

Fewer guests meant less work, which she was grateful for considering she and Sybil were currently splitting Claudia's housekeeping and laundry chores on top of their own. Fewer guests also meant less potential help with the harvesting.

So far though, Solo was handling the farm work more efficiently than five men could. It was nice to have a healthy, reliable man staying long term at Falls Creek. Someone vibrant and agile, unlike her father and Leonard.

She paused by the sink as the feeling of sitting with Solo on the porch last night warmed her heart. It felt comfortable to relax beside him on the swing, knowing he cared about the inn, about her.

There was more to him than she'd first thought. He was once just another guest to her, then an unwelcome long-term boarder. But once he saved Leonard's life and the harvest, everything changed. She could depend on him.

And unlike most of the people she'd depended on in her life, Solo hadn't left… yet.

Last night on the porch swing, she'd wondered about his family, his childhood, how he got the scar on his eyebrow, if he had a sweetheart somewhere. But she hadn't asked. The quiet had been too nice to shatter with conversation, her tongue too tired to form unnecessary words. All that was needed was the peace between them and the lovely way it opened her heart. She was starting to care for him too. He would make a wonderful father for Zeke.

She nearly dropped the dish at the thought. She couldn't think that way. Shouldn't. Maybe it was just the warmth off the stove that was flushing heat to her face. Yes, that was all. She'd been overworked and overwhelmed, so of course she had enjoyed the few relaxing moments on the porch swing with a caring man who was doing ninety percent of the farm and stable managing for no pay. That didn't mean they would get married and be a family.

These feelings swirling inside her weren't romantic sentiment. Not at all. Couldn't be. She'd promised her heart to Ezekiel forever, and loving anyone else would break that promise. Her heart wasn't strong enough to love twice.

Or was it?

Zeke ran into the house through the side door, commanding Eva's attention. He was carrying a basket of

Claudia and Leonard's dirty dishes. He hefted the basket onto the countertop by the sink. "Here you go, Mama."

"Thanks, love."

"Mama?"

"Hm?"

"Do I have to do school lessons this afternoon? I want to play outside with Benny."

Eva glanced out the window over the sink. The young boy whose family was staying at the inn was running across the yard by the greenhouse. He appeared to be a head taller than Zeke, but his parents said he was only eight. Zeke rarely had a chance to play with boys even close to his age. The two had chatted incessantly throughout lunch, warming her heart. She smiled at her son. "I suppose it wouldn't hurt to skip your lessons for one day. You may go play with your new friend."

He beamed widely, revealing a sliver of white breaking through the space in his gums where he'd lost his front tooth. She bent down to have a closer look. "Your first adult tooth is finally coming in. It looks very handsome."

He was too excited about going to play to care about a tooth. "I know. Bye, Mama!" he said, as he ran out of the kitchen.

Sybil chuckled as she scrubbed the stove. "Sweet boy."

As Zeke dashed for the side door, Frederick was walking down the hall. He stopped in the doorway and pointed at Zeke. "Where is he going in such a fired-up hurry?"

Eva scraped the fish bones off another dish. "To play with his new friend."

Frederick nodded briskly. "Well, I'm heading out to the cottage to check on Revel."

"Leonard, you mean."

Frederick started to walk away then turned back and looked at her. He scratched his white beard. "Leonard?"

"Yes, Leonard."

"Who is Leonard?"

Eva's stomach sank. She set the dish down and wiped her hands on her apron, trying to look unconcerned even though she wanted to tell her father to go sit in the comfy chair in the reception room and not get up. "You said you will check on Revel, but you meant Leonard. It's your cousin Leonard who is in the cottage recovering from a stroke. He and Claudia have lived there for over forty years."

Frederick looked out the screen door, his voice barely above a whisper. "Then where is Revel?"

She slowly stepped toward her father and put a hand on his arm. "Your son Revel is living in Good Springs while he works with Connor Bradshaw. Remember, John Colburn is boarding him?"

He peeled her hand off his arm. "Don't treat me like a child."

"Father, I—"

"I'm seventy years old—"

"Seventy-two."

"And I don't need you treating me like a child."

It would only upset him if she defended herself, so she simply nodded.

Her father squared his shoulders and walked outside. She stood at the kitchen window, watching to make sure he made it to the cottage.

Sybil gave her a sad look and met her by the window. "He is getting worse, isn't he?"

A catch in Eva's throat kept her silent. Her chin tightened. Sybil leaned her head against Eva's shoulder and they stared out the window silently like they often did after Revel left and their mother left. And after Ezekiel died.

Neither said a word nor did they need to. The sweet and sad intimacy of knowing and being known without words conveyed more than all the volumes in the world. She'd felt a glimpse of that intimacy with Solo last night too.

Just the thought of his care for her shined a ray of light into her shadowy heart. It was a hope she could pass on to Sybil. She gave her sister a kiss on the top of her head. "We will be fine, Syb. We will watch out for Father and mind the inn the best we can till Revel comes home. Isaac Owens will move here soon, and we have Solo with us for a while longer." Only sixteen days to be exact. But who was counting?

She was. With dread. And not just because he was helping with the farm work.

Sybil wiped her tears with a knuckle and returned to scrubbing the stove.

Eva thought of Revel and how he should be here. How he'd abandoned his responsibilities and was off having his adventures while his family suffered. Surely, the honorable Reverend John Colburn didn't know the whole story or he wouldn't be harboring Revel and enabling this breach of tradition.

It was time she wrote to Good Springs' overseer and let him know he needed to send Revel home to the inn.

She brushed her hands on her apron. "I'll be in my office if you need me."

The lady of the family who was staying in Room 5 had claimed a headache after lunch. Her off-pitch singing was bleeding down the stairs. She must not feel too badly.

Eva closed her office door to muffle the sound and sat at her desk. She drew her pen from its holder and wrote. *Dear Mr. Colburn—*

A light knock rattled the door.

"Come in."

Solo stepped inside, holding his hat in one hand. He smelled like the sunshine and had dust on his boots, as a man did when he'd worked the first half of the day. "I was headed out to the stables to check on the foals, but I saw your door was shut so—"

"So you came to check on me instead."

A boyish grin humbled his expression. "Something like that."

Once again, his concern touched her heart. A wave of emotion deepened her breath. She tried to tamp it down. "That was thoughtful of you. But as you can see, I'm perfectly fine." She stood as if that proved her strength.

His unbroken gaze pierced her soul. At once her hands felt awkward. She folded them in front of her and tried to think of something to say.

After a long moment, he motioned to Zeke's schoolbooks on the side table by the door. "No reading lessons this afternoon?"

"Since Zeke has someone to play with, I gave him the afternoon off school."

"You made the right choice."

Though she didn't need his approval, it was nice to have someone agree with her. "Most people would say he should be learning, not playing."

Solo shook his head casually. "I think children learn best while playing."

She wanted to talk more and not just because his kind gaze drew her in. Her mind wondered what other childrearing techniques they might agree upon. As she studied him, her heart filled with guilt.

She snapped her attention away from his stubble-covered jaw and motioned to her desk. "I just came in here to write a quick letter before I tend to the rooms upstairs."

"You don't owe me an explanation." He cocked his chin and a slow smile curved his lips. "Sit and breathe for as long as you need to. You work harder than any woman I've ever known."

"Sit and breathe," she repeated with a little laugh. "I still have to clean two guest rooms. Sybil will finish the laundry this afternoon, but I have to make the beds while she starts supper." She rubbed her temples. "It's selfish of me, but I'm ready for Claudia to come back to work."

He caught her anxious fingertips in his hand. "No, not selfish. It's understandable. You can only do so much in a day."

The heat from his skin permeated hers. He traced a callused thumb over her knuckles. Her eyes begged to look away but were held captive by his gaze. Her words came out on stunted breath. "I thought I wanted to be alone, but after last night I…"

He leaned an inch closer, his voice low and smooth. "You what?"

"I realized I'm tired of being alone. Feeling alone. I'm surrounded by people all the time here but still feel… alone. I have since my mother left and Revel left and Ezekiel died." Something flashed behind Solo's eyes when she said her late husband's name. She wanted to ask why but didn't. "It's even harder to be alone now that Zeke is growing up and needs more than I can give."

He narrowed his hazel eyes briefly. "Don't say that. You're a great mother. You give him everything he needs."

"He needs a father." The words slipped out faster than she could stop them. For a fraction of a second she hoped maybe she hadn't said it aloud, but the easy grin returned to one corner of his mouth.

His unrelenting gaze finally left her eyes. It traveled to her lips, draining the power from her resolve. Something gripped her insides like when she was a child and would swing from the rope over the creek and fly into the water. Or when she would race her horse across the paddock and jump the back fence. Or when she was sixteen and a trader's handsome son took her behind the barn to kiss her. She'd married him three years later. She was still in love with him, so how could she stand this close to another man, letting him hold her hand and look at her lips?

The second she thought it, Solo's gaze shot back up to her eyes. "You don't have to be alone anymore." He lowered his mouth to hers and kissed her once, slowly and gently then pulled back, his breath on her skin. "I won't leave Falls Creek until you tell me to."

She watched his mouth as he released her hand and took a step back. Her chin still tingled from the scratch of his whiskers.

He put his hat on and tipped the brim to her. "I'll be in the stables. See you at suppertime."

He closed her office door, and immediately she touched her lips and melted into her chair. In the distance outside her window, the big gray leaf tree's shadow darkened the yard around the iron bench by Ezekiel's gravestone. She stood and yanked the curtains closed, but it did nothing to stop the guilt pulsing through her torn heart.

CHAPTER TWENTY

Adrip of sweat ran down Bailey's forehead, tickling her eyebrow. She wiped it with the back of her hand. Packing hay into a barn loft was the best workout she'd had in years. The muscles between her shoulder blades burned pleasurably. Every plunge and lift of the pitchfork demanded her muscles contract, and when they released, the built-up stress and sorrow poured out with her sweat.

Thanks to John and the guys for letting her join their work, she hadn't focused on her loss as much as she had while sitting idly in the house. When she kept her body moving, her mind had something real and raw to concentrate on. Emotional pain was just as real and raw, but it didn't help to think about it.

As she took a swig from her water bottle, John called to her from outside the loft window. "It will be awhile before Connor and Revel return with another load of hay."

"I'll be ready."

"Take a break. Come with me to the house for a drink of water."

She held up her water bottle. "I still have plenty."

John knocked his hat's brim higher with a knuckle and looked up at her from fifteen feet below. "You should take a break. Lydia was worried about your being up there doing men's work again today."

Seeing as how the good doctor was the first female physician in the Land, Bailey doubted it was Lydia who was worried about the work being too demanding for a female. "I'm fine, John." She leaned her palms on the splintery window ledge, and the fresh air hit her face. "Lydia knows this is good for me."

John took off his hat and wiped his forehead with a handkerchief then walked toward the house. Sweat sealed his shirt to his back. He was the hardest working pastor Bailey had ever met. Everyone here in the Land seemed to work hard. It felt right.

She threw her pitchfork like a javelin at the stack of hay across the loft. It stuck in the cured grass and stood upright. She left it there and clipped her water bottle's carabiner to her belt loop then climbed down the ladder to the barn floor.

Two of the family's four horses were in their stalls. One had its rump facing the stall gate. The other lifted its nose at her when she passed. She recognized it from the night she came to the Land, the night she'd lost Tim.

The breeze wafted through the barn's double wide doorway. Outside, the sun warmed her skin as much as the air cooled it. It was only the fourth week of autumn in the Land, but everyone here spoke as if the season would be short.

She took another drink of water. It was too pleasant an afternoon to go inside, and if she sat quietly, her mind would wander backward instead of forward. Living in the past would lead to depression in the same way that living in the future led to anxiety. Somehow she had to stay in the moment. Instead of following John to the house, she ambled to the other side of the barn, wanting privacy but staying close so she would be ready when Revel and Connor came back with another load of hay.

This work was good for her, and she intended to finish the day's chores with the men. Not only did she need to stay busy, she needed to earn her keep. Once she had left her final foster family on her eighteenth birthday, she told herself never to be dependent on strangers again.

She leaned against the barn and rested for only a moment. As disheartening memories threatened to flood back, a pile of scrap lumber beside the fire pit caught her eye. Sandy gravel crunched under her shoes as she hurried to the burn pile. The boards waiting for the next fire were unfit for building, but they were solid and dry. Just how she liked them.

She picked out two thick boards and carried them to a tree stump then toed off her shoes. Propping the first board at an angle between the ground and the stump, she settled her bare feet into the dry grass. After blowing out a slow breath, she sent a front snap kick into the board, splitting it in half. The resounding crack of wood energized her system. She tossed the broken pieces back onto the burn pile and set up the second board. It cracked as easily as the first.

After rummaging through the old wood, she returned to the stump with a half dozen boards. She used her left foot to break the next board, but the fun of the challenge was wearing off. If she ever looked bored in front of Coach, he had a remedy. She did what he would have done and stacked two boards at once for the next kick.

She settled her breath and concentrated on the doubly thick wood, focusing on the exact spot where she needed to strike to split both boards at once. It was about the thickness of the closet door she'd been locked behind by one of her foster moms when the military men came around. She would never be trapped like that again.

With a surge of energy, she snapped both pieces of wood in two. Their crack echoed off the barn.

If she could break two at once, why not try three?

She threw the broken pieces back to the burn pile like flying discs and then set up the last three good boards in one thick stack against the stump. It had been years since she'd attempted to break three boards at once. She slowed her breathing and steadied her focus as she had for the other breaks. "Be strong," she whispered just as she'd told herself in that dark closet twenty years ago. She hadn't known how to break a door down then, but she did now.

With all her might she kicked the center of the boards. They snapped and collapsed into a defeated stack on the ground.

A slow clap of applause came from behind her. She turned to see Connor approaching. He smirked. "Nicely done."

Great. That was all she needed—the chief of the plowboy police watching her break boards. She cleaned up the broken wood. "Did you enjoy the show?"

After tossing the first two boards into the pile, she reached for the others, but Connor was holding one, examining it.

He pointed to the splintered edge. "You cracked this board clean through a knot in the wood."

"So?"

"That isn't easy." His smirk was gone. "Black belt?"

"Second degree."

"Had a feeling." He tossed the wood into the burn pile. It smacked the rest of her discards. He straightened his spine and stood, towering over her. "We could use another skilled fighter on the security team."

All that was calm within her began to rumble. She would not let this former warrior rattle her. So what if he looked and sounded and stood like the men who'd been on the other side of that closet door? This man wasn't a threat. He was John Colburn's trusted son-in-law, and he was offering her a challenge. But one she couldn't accept. She stepped back. "Your security team is the reason I'm alone here."

Connor crossed his arms, the lines of his shoulders making a strong square. "We were training to protect our land when your crewmen opened fire."

"*Our* land?" she repeated.

"Yes, this is my home now. Has been for years." His furrowed brow relaxed and he uncrossed his arms. "And, Bailey, I've found a person is never alone in the Land. Come to training tonight. I think my guys could learn a lot from you." He lifted his chin at the barn. "We train in there. Nineteen hundred hours."

CHAPTER TWENTY-ONE

Solo relaxed into the back of the wooden chair and studied Frederick and Zeke from across the dinner table. The young boy only resembled his grandfather when he made a stern face at his puppy, which was currently pulling on his sock beneath the table. Zeke must have inherited his father's features because nothing about him looked like his mother except the color of his dark brown eyes.

Zeke would be an easy boy to raise. With little effort Solo could imagine adopting him. He already cared for Zeke and wanted to protect him and teach him and help Eva bring him up in the Lord. Hopefully, Zeke wouldn't be their only child.

No matter how much Solo tried to rein in his thoughts, after kissing Eva today, he'd wondered more than once what it would be like to have a family with her.

Eva zipped past as she cleared dishes from the guests' tables. Solo hoped to catch her eye and steal a smile, but she moved away too quickly. Maybe once she was done with work she would slow down long enough to see the desire in his eyes. Perhaps she knew it was there and was trying to avoid it.

Heavens, he hoped not.

Yes, he yearned for her but with a desire that was far beyond physical. He wanted to know everything about her, and he wanted her to know she was loved.

The family from Pleasant Valley rose from their seats, thanked Eva for the meal, and left the dining hall with the lethargy of people who'd spent the day working and playing out-of-doors. A moment later, the two traders who'd helped with the harvesting all day also trudged upstairs. Since no new guests had come to the inn today, it was just the family and Solo left in the dining hall.

Frederick hummed one grateful note as he scraped the last bite of apple pie from his plate. He perched his wrinkled elbows on the table. "Fine meal tonight, Peach," he said to Eva when she returned to clear their table.

"I'm glad you enjoyed it."

Solo watched her lips as she spoke to her father. Zeke was in the middle of telling them about playing with his new friend in the yard all afternoon. Solo didn't hear much of what he said either. All he could do was watch Eva and think of their kiss.

Sybil's excited voice rejoiced in the kitchen, drawing everyone's attention. "Hallelujah!" She marched into the dining hall with Claudia, who was smiling for the first time since Leonard's stroke. "Praise the Lord!" she exclaimed as she strode to the family's table.

Frederick straightened his posture. "What's happened?"

"Leonard stood!" Claudia glanced from Frederick to Eva and then Solo. "He stood up after dinner and took a few steps."

Frederick clapped once, beaming like Zeke did when he first got the puppy.

Now Solo could see the resemblance.

Eva set down the dirty dishes and wrapped Claudia in a hug. "How wonderful!"

"Indeed!" Claudia wiped a happy tear from her cheek. "It wore him plumb out, but he did it."

Zeke looked at Solo from across the table. "Does that mean Leonard will be all right?"

Solo weighed his words, unsure of what it meant medically, seeing as how the doctor hadn't thought Leonard would recover at all. "It means God can do more than we expect Him to."

Frederick nodded. "Quite right, Solo. Quite right. Let's celebrate!" He pointed at a shelf over the mantel where their games were kept. "Zeke, scare up a deck of cards over there, and we'll enjoy ourselves tonight. Care to stay for a game, Claudia?"

"No, I want to get back to the cottage in case Leonard needs me."

Eva walked out of the dining hall with her, their happy conversation continuing.

Zeke jumped from his chair, and his little dog yapped once as it chased him across the room to the game shelf. After rummaging through a stack of paper boxes and thin boards, he ran back to the table with a red box of playing cards. "Can we play Pairs?"

Frederick began shuffling the cards. "Just until your mama and Sybil finish cleaning up, then I'll teach you an old game we can all play together." He gave Solo a wink. "It's called Bluff."

Zeke sat on his knees in his chair and wiggled with excitement as they played Pairs. His pile of pairs grew faster than his grandfather's and Solo's, but both men were too happy to mind being beaten by a six-year-old—Frederick elated over the news of Leonard's recovery and Solo over the affection he felt for Eva.

They were halfway through their third game of Pairs when Eva and Sybil came out of the kitchen. Each lady had shed her apron and looked tired but pretty. As they approached the table, Solo stood and pulled out the chair next to him for Eva.

Her cheeks flushed slightly. "Thank you."

"My pleasure," he said as he sat beside her, inhaling her feminine scent.

Sybil sat by Zeke and frequently glanced at Solo then gave Eva an odd look. Maybe Sybil knew about the kiss. The sisters probably talked about everything in their lives, including men. Whenever he looked up from his cards, Sybil shifted her eyes between him and Eva. Yes, the younger sister definitely knew he'd kissed Eva. She had him beat though because he didn't know how Eva felt about the kiss, about him.

Fair enough. He would let the sisters have their secrets for now because one day he would marry Eva and be a part of this family. One day he would know how Eva felt because he would be her husband and would devote his life to knowing her. But for now, he was enjoying the mystery.

If Eva hadn't liked what happened in the office today, she wouldn't be sitting beside him now. She wouldn't have told her sister enough to make the woman glance at him and smile demurely every couple of minutes. Just when he thought he might never know how Eva felt, her leg sidled up against his under the table. If she didn't feel something for him, she certainly wouldn't have done that.

As the game continued, Solo lost every hand he played—not because he was bad at Bluff. But what man could concentrate when he was overwhelmed by a woman's furtive touch, especially if it was the woman he loved?

Love. It was the muse of poets and playwrights, and he was neither. He was a simple horse breeder who had a few children's stories to write, and he couldn't even do that like he'd planned. Oh, he could, but then he'd be missing out on the ecstasy of falling for a woman who might be falling for him too.

His children's book would have to wait. He would write those stories and more one day for Zeke and for any future children he and Eva were blessed with. It didn't matter that he'd worked for most of his forty days at Falls Creek because he was no longer counting the days.

He'd told Eva he wouldn't leave the inn until she said to, and he meant it. He would stay and do Leonard's job until the new man started. Then he would take over for Frederick if the older man would have him.

Yes, Eva's search for a new stable manager was over. He was the man for her in more ways than one. She just didn't know it yet. He would make a life here with Eva and her son. Telling her now would probably put her on guard, so he would woo her gently. She deserved to be lulled softly and loved fiercely, and he was the man to do it.

CHAPTER TWENTY-TWO

Bailey shoved her hands into her pockets as she walked through the dewy grass toward the barn. The night air had cooled quickly after the sun set. Her back was tired from a long day of physical labor and her belly was full from dinner. She wanted to relax, but she'd been invited to take part in something she was good at. This was her chance to connect with these people. She couldn't let it matter that looking at Connor reminded her of all she wanted to forget.

Before opening the barn door, she stood under the eave and listened to the men inside. Connor was counting like a drill sergeant, and each number was followed by a burst of baritone grunts. It reminded her of training with Coach and the team when she was younger. She opened the barn door without knocking, tossed her Eastern Shore University sweatshirt onto a workbench, and joined the men doing push-ups in the middle of the barn floor.

The room was dimly lit by an oil lantern hanging from the rafters. Something wet squished under her right hand, and every time she lowered her body, her nose almost touched a clump of horse manure. She missed the matt-covered floor in Coach's well-lit gym in Virginia but couldn't let it distract her. This was her life now, horse manure and all.

Connor gushed out air. "Fifty!" He shot up to his bare feet as did the five other men in the room. They looked like Civil War era civilian farmers training with their local militia, but Connor had taught them modern fitness and form. Masculine energy pulsed through the ripe barn.

Bailey followed Connor's lead as the former navy pilot continued the warm up. After a few minutes of star jumps he stopped and stretched his neck to both sides. While the other guys panted, Connor looked at Bailey. "I told them you would join us tonight."

When he'd invited her this afternoon, she'd declined. Neither had mentioned it at dinner. "How did you know I would come?"

He flashed a confident grin. "Just knew."

If he didn't posture himself so much like the enemy of her childhood, she could see why Lydia liked him. He was almost charming. It didn't stop her from wanting to kick him in the face.

She glanced at the other men in the barn's open center. Revel stood to her right, red faced and sweaty. She recognized three of the others from the beach. Levi Colburn looked just like John but was thirty years younger and twenty pounds bulkier than his dad. Lanky sheep farmer Everett Foster flipped his dark hair off his forehead and began shadow boxing, already hyped for whatever they would do next. He was recently married to Bethany, John's youngest daughter. That much Bailey had gleaned from dinner conversations.

Bailey hadn't met the other two men but recognized one from the beach. He was Nicholas Vestal, Sophia's boyfriend. She'd never seen the man who was standing farthest from the door, but he probably had some sort of Colburn connection. Was there any way not to be connected in a society descended from eight families?

Connor raked his black hair off his forehead. "Tonight, we will work on blocking. Bailey is a second-degree black belt in martial arts. She was a competitive fighter back in the day." He sent her a wink. "Let's see if you've still got it."

She toed off her shoes and met Connor in the center of the barn's smooth dirt floor. The five other men stepped back into a semicircle, giving them space. Connor put his hand on her shoulder while he addressed the men. She let him get away with it for the sake of comradery.

"I haven't had the pleasure of sparring with Bailey yet, but if she's as good as I think she is, this will be the best demonstration of blocking I can give you." He removed his hand and looked down at her. "Sixty seconds. Give me all you got, Jeans."

She ignored his attempt to nickname her by the pants she wore and matched his smirk. "You asked for it."

Connor glanced at Levi, who pulled out a pocket watch. "One minute." Then he took a step backward into a stance from a martial arts style differing from her training.

She took her stance, unsure what rules—if any—they were to follow. He'd said they were going to demonstrate blocking. Who was supposed to strike and who would block? If she were back in Coach's gym, he'd tell her to be ready, to be strong.

Connor's expression darkened as he prepared to fight. "Go."

She gave a quick bow out of habit, but instead of bouncing with energy, she stayed where she was and analyzed his movements as he approached. His jaw was set a fraction to the left, and his right foot turned outward more than the other when he walked. She could use his structural imbalance to her favor, but his extra six inches of stature would enable him to reach her first.

He threw an easy straight punch at the center of her chest, testing her. She slipped to the side using only the controlled movement of her waist to avoid him. His fist flew past her. He repeated the punch, then again, alternating left and right, coming faster with each attempt to strike. She added a bob to her weave and evaded every punch, not having to risk contact.

If this was supposed to be a blocking demonstration, the men might think she was a poor teacher, but Connor wasn't throwing anything she couldn't avoid. Coach's voice was embedded in her mind. *Avoidance is always better than contact.*

Connor bent his knees as if resetting his balance to change his approach. There was no way he was getting tired already. When he leaned back on his dominant foot, she stopped bobbing and anticipated his kick. If he wanted her to block it, he was in for a surprise. With a quick bend of her waist, she dipped and swung her upper body, allowing the momentum to make her flip and land behind him.

He didn't lose his balance as she'd expected but turned, challenge burning in his eyes, and attacked. His fists whooshed air across her face. He'd been holding back before. Probably thought he was playing with a little girl. She wasn't a little girl anymore, scared of the drunken military men her foster moms brought home.

And she was done avoiding contact with Connor Bradshaw.

She wove to the side one last time, and as he pulled his fist back she attacked. He blocked her first kick with lightning reflexes and was ready for the second. He must have known her form from watching her break boards earlier in the day.

She had underestimated him. Still, she was on the offensive and fired off every punch and kick combination drilled into her by a coach who wanted her to be able to fight off aggressive men.

With Connor's every block, her anger grew. He deserved to be hit, to be beaten into the ground. Him and every guy like him. She punched harder and faster, but he blocked her every attempt.

"Time!" Levi yelled.

Her disciplined muscles immediately disengaged as did Connor's. She stepped back and bowed sharply even though she wanted to throw one last kick. Connor nodded his version of a bow. The darkness receded from his eyes as quickly as it had come.

The dusty barn fell silent except for her and Connor's heavy breath. He put both hands behind his head and let out an exhilarated whoop then grinned. "She's better than I thought she would be."

As he explained their differing tactics to the guys, all Bailey could hear was the angry blood pumping past her eardrums. His measured military tone made her want to jump back in front of him and ram his nose into his brain.

What had come over her? Maybe it was years of built-up frustration finally having a chance at release and not landing a solid punch. Maybe she wasn't ready for this. Whatever it was, she had to get out of here.

Grabbing her sweatshirt from the workbench, she left the barn as quickly and wordlessly as she had entered. The chilly air did little to cool her while she stormed to the house. A lone cricket chirped in the ankle-high grass outside, singing its monotone ballad to the dark night sky. It paused its music as she passed by.

The kitchen door was closed, which meant someone in the house was already in bed. Probably Lydia. She'd been up all last night, delivering someone's baby, and had looked like she was about to fall asleep at dinner. Just three weeks ago Bailey had been Lydia's patient, and now she knew the family's routine. Her life was changing by the day, but not how she'd expected.

Through the door's window she could see a table lantern burning softly in the kitchen. John was good about leaving a light on for his busy household even after he'd gone upstairs for the night. He'd given her a bedroom and a seat at his table, but this beautiful old house in no way felt like home—whatever that feeling was supposed to be.

Bailey reached for the doorknob and as she gripped it, pain stabbed through her hand. She stepped into the warm kitchen and examined her fingers in the lantern light. Her right pinkie had been jammed during her spar with Connor. Now that she noticed, it began to throb.

Footsteps shuffled into the kitchen and a man's voice came from the doorway behind her. "Are you all right?"

She didn't look Revel in the eye but reached to the cabinet for a water cup, using only her left hand so he wouldn't see her jammed finger. "I'm fine." She turned to the sink and pressed the pedal beneath it to fill the cup. "Did Connor send you to check on me?"

"No, I came on my own."

"You shouldn't have." She took a drink of water, but it didn't quench her thirst. "I don't need people checking up on me."

Revel stepped closer. "Because you are fine."

"That's right."

He leaned casually against the edge of the porcelain sink. "Do you hate me and Connor and the other guys because of what happened on the shore, or have you always hated men?"

It was the opposite, actually. She'd always gotten along better with guys, even as a child. The girls at school never welcomed a foster kid with mismatched clothes, but the boys didn't care as long as she was good at sports. Then once she started training at the dojo, most of her friends were guys. "I don't hate anyone." She tipped the water cup higher and let the last few drops slide down her throat. "Especially guys."

He raised his thick, brown eyebrows. "Any woman who wants to pummel a man as badly as you tried with Connor must have a problem with men." He lowered his volume as he had the morning they both were in the kitchen before sunrise. "Who hurt you, Bailey? Was it your father?"

The simple suspenders-wearing man was more perceptive than she'd given him credit for. Even though he'd been at the beach that fateful night, he didn't seem like one of *them* to her. Maybe because he was new to the Colburn house. She and Revel had that in common. Cool water poured into her cup as she refilled it. "I don't have a father."

Revel tilted his chin down and short strands of sweaty hair fell across his forehead. "Everyone has a father."

"Not me."

"Just because you're angry with the man doesn't mean he doesn't exist."

"Nope, no dad to be angry with. Check my birth certificate."

He pushed his damp hair back, sadness shadowing his face. "Oh. I'm sorry. Sounds like a perfect reason to want to pummel the entire sex."

He seemed to be struggling with this more than she was. Perhaps it was time she clued him in enough to give him peace so he'd leave her alone. "Have you ever seen a woman spar an opponent before?"

He chuckled. "Not unless you call my sisters' childhood catfights sparring."

"I don't."

"Then no."

"That's why you mistook my focus and determination for hatred. It was competition, that's all." It wasn't, but she hadn't had a chance to figure out her own emotions during the impromptu match. There was no way she would sort out her feelings with this guy. "You've never seen a woman in battle before. We're fierce. So you can go back to training now and tell Connor I'm fine."

He looked down at her injured hand and his expression changed. "Oh, I see the problem." He gently took her injured hand in his and turned it toward the light. "This is why you're doing everything with your left hand."

She shrugged. "I'm ambidextrous."

"No, you aren't. I just watched you fight Connor. You're right handed." He met her gaze then returned his focus to her swollen finger joint. "Can you bend it?"

"Yeah, it's fine."

"It's fine. You're fine," he repeated her frequent expression as he slowly pulled on her pinkie, relieving the pressure.

"I can do that for myself." Even though she spoke the words, she didn't take her hand away from him.

"No one should have to do this for themselves."

"Do you know how many times I jammed fingers in my years of training?"

"Probably as many times as I've jammed mine in the last few weeks training with Connor." He released her hand then walked to the wide doorway and leaned into the living room. "John, do we have any ice?"

John's calm voice came from the other room. "The ice box is in the cellar. What is wrong?"

"Bailey hurt her hand."

"Take a lantern. The steps are steep. There should be a pick on top of the icebox."

While Revel carried a chamber lantern outside to go down to the cellar, John walked into the kitchen and gave Bailey a compassionate look. "Do you need to see Lydia?"

"No, it's just a jammed finger." She sat in the ladder-back chair at the end of the long wooden table. "I've hurt it before. I'm fine."

"Injuries in our youth cause the most pain when we age." John yawned. "I must retire for the evening. You should get some rest too." He put his hand on her shoulder and closed his eyes. "Lord, I pray You comfort Bailey with Your peace and Your healing. May she learn to trust You fully." With a short pat, he removed his caring hand then shuffled up the stairs.

Bailey sat frozen in the chair. Coach used to pray for the whole team before a competition, but no one had prayed for her before bed since the summer she spent at the Polk family's house in the country when she was ten. Scenes from every obstacle she'd faced in the sixteen years since flashed through her mind like a reel of tragic highlights. Yet through it all, God had guided her, carried her even, to this place. If she'd never stayed with the Polk family, she wouldn't have faith in God. Nor would she have gone to college to major in plant biology. If she hadn't been in Professor Tim's class, she never would have been able to work with him on PharmaTech projects, which led to her being contacted by Justin Mercer, which led to her coming to the Land, to this place where people touched her easily and cared about her and prayed for her.

She surveyed the lantern lit country kitchen with its warm stone hearth and beamed ceiling. This was all she'd wanted; this was where it all led. So why was she still fighting?

She didn't want to fight anymore. She didn't know what she wanted her life to be like in the Land, but she wanted peace. Martial arts would always be a part of her life for fitness but not for the fight. That's why sparring with Connor had made her angry. She wasn't mad at him or the other men on the security team. It was a matter of being dragged back into a life she needed to leave behind—a life of inviting threat to prove she could survive.

Revel rounded the kitchen doorway and walked to the table. He held the lantern by its finger loop and had a chunk of ice in the other hand. "This should help."

His kindness touched her heart. "You didn't have to do that."

"Yes, I did." He wrapped the ice in a tea towel and crouched in front of her. "Put this over your knuckle and leave it there for a quarter hour."

"I've got this, really. You should go back to the barn." She held up her swollen finger. "This isn't worth mentioning to the guys."

That got a quick smile out of him. "I won't say anything. Connor probably already knows. He doesn't miss much."

"Yeah, I figured."

"He's a good man." He pressed his lips together in a solemn line while he stood. "You'll see that once you get to know him."

Before Revel made it to the door, Bailey stopped him. "Revel?"

He turned and looked at her with expectant eyes.

She hadn't wanted his attention nor his concern, but now that he was leaving, some immature part of her wanted him to come back to the table and talk. She swallowed the girlish feeling and held up the cloth-wrapped ice. "Thank you."

CHAPTER TWENTY-THREE

After sweeping the dining hall floor, Eva gently closed the screen door and walked down the four wooden steps from the side porch to the lawn. Dry grass crackled under her boot heels. The big gray leaf tree on the east side of the inn cast its afternoon shadow over the graveyard and beckoned her to sit on the iron bench and relax.

As she ambled toward the bench, the autumn wind blew loose strands of hair away from her neck and chilled her sweaty skin. Over the past week, Leonard had gained the strength to walk to the house for lunch each day; and afterward while he napped on the divan in the reception room, Claudia hummed as she cleaned vacant guest rooms upstairs.

Finally, Eva's afternoons had regained an occasional, peaceful lull, but whenever her hands were still, her mind raced.

Revel hadn't replied to her last message. Nor had John Colburn, but she'd only sent her letters a week ago. The trader might not have made it to Good Springs yet, especially if he'd stayed more than a night in Woodland.

No matter how pressing her needs to get Revel to come home and to hire another man, her thoughts mostly centered on Solo. He had spent the week bringing in the harvest and managing the stables, always whistling, always moving. He'd become adept at supervising the traders who worked to pay their board. Or maybe he'd already possessed those skills before coming to Falls Creek and she hadn't known.

There was much she didn't know about Solomon Cotter, and they hadn't spoken about his past, which both scared and intrigued her. Since the day he kissed her in the office, she often took breaks while cleaning upstairs to stop at the windows and look out over the property, hoping to spot him. Often, she did. Zeke was usually with him, one or both of them smiling.

She put her arm across the back of the iron bench and looked back at the distant horse paddock. Zeke sat atop Solo's black draft horse named King, and Solo was walking beside them, leading the animal. A twinge of fear at seeing her little boy on such a big horse caught her breath. She shouldn't worry; Solo wouldn't let anything happen to Zeke.

She looked away and her gaze landed on the tombstone. Here she was admiring the man who was teaching her son to ride a horse, and her late husband rested in his grave, having never known his son existed.

Half of her heart told her eyes not to look back at Solo, but the other half warmed with affection for the man who'd saved the harvest, who'd ridden for hours to get the doctor for Leonard, who'd awakened her soul. He'd come to the inn to write children's stories yet ended up spending his few spare moments teaching her child life skills. Just like a father.

Of course, she admired Solo. And he made his attraction clear by kissing her, by helping her, by the way he kept his eyes on her through every meal while she served the guests.

The wind picked up speed and tossed a wisp of hair across her face. She turned away from the touching scene in the paddock and looked down at Ezekiel's headstone. Her heart stung with guilt.

She used to feel grief when she came here and assumed the grief equated her love. She still loved him, but the grief lessened with time. Now, guilt overshadowed the waning grief. With Solo in her life, she was no longer lonely, and the grief had almost vanished. Did that mean her love for Ezekiel had lessened too?

And so the guilt grew.

The screen door banged, and Frederick stepped out of the inn. As her father hobbled toward the bench, Eva scooted down to make room for him. He grunted when he sat. "Haven't seen you sit out here for a while, Peach."

"I haven't had the time. But now that Claudia is back to work, I—"

"It isn't Claudia who has made the difference for you."

"Pardon?"

"It's Solo."

She glanced at the paddock where Solo was helping Zeke dismount the horse. Her stomach relaxed, relieved her son was safely standing on the ground. "Yes, Solomon has been a big help around here."

Frederick shook his head once. "Not what I meant, and you know it."

He didn't speak again. There was never a comfortable silence between them as there was with her and Sybil…

or her and Solo. No matter how old she was, her father knew how to make her talk. He picked at invisible lint on his sleeve while he waited for her to take the bait.

She blew out a jagged breath. "I promised Ezekiel forever. You were there."

"I remember your wedding clearer than yesterday. You said until death do you part." He raised a crooked finger toward the headstone. "You and Ezekiel have parted, Peach."

"I know." The words slipped out reflexively. She'd spent nearly seven years reciting her promise as if it kept them together. It had given her widowhood a noble quality, but now it seemed empty—like her heart before Solo stirred whatever this was inside her, confusing her, condemning her.

Zeke's laughter drifted on the air as he skipped out of the paddock with his puppy running behind him. Her little boy followed Solo while he walked King toward the stable's archway. Solo held out the rope to Zeke and let him lead the horse. Zeke took it proudly.

Frederick lifted his chin at them. "He's right for the job."

"Zeke?" She chuckled. "Let's give him a few years to grow up first."

"You know who I'm talking about. He's got the hay put up, the harvest brought in, and the cows are milked twice a day. He's even sharpened and oiled half the tools in the barn. He's the man for the job."

Those were all farm duties—Leonard's duties. Just when she thought her father was in his right mind, he seemed to be slipping away again. "No, Father. We've already hired Isaac Owens for the farm manager job."

"Not for that. For my job."

"You want me to hire Solo to be the stable manager?"

"Like I said, he's the right man for the job." He scratched his white beard. "And not just that job. He's the right man for you too."

"Father—"

"Don't sass me, Peach."

She didn't respond but let her vision wander as she stared across the property. A man from Stonehill who'd been working with Solo in the stables for several days walked out of the barn and toward the bunkhouse. Eva pointed at him. "Sam is interested in the job. He has good experience and I've already talked to him about moving out here. He said he could turn the empty storage room on the south wing of the stable block into a room for himself."

"Solo could too. He's a good man."

"Yes, he is a good man. That's not the point." The myriad reasons Solo shouldn't move to Falls Creek rolled off her tongue. "He has lived in Riverside his whole life. He has a job there at the ranch. They're probably wanting him back by now."

"I think a change would do him good."

"He's good at what he does. If he wants to change employers, I'm sure he could make a fine living working for himself. He didn't plan to stay here permanently. He only came here to write his stories. Since he's had no time for that, he probably wants to leave as soon he can." As she said the words, she remembered how he said he wouldn't leave Falls Creek until she told him to. The look in his eyes had rooted its way into her heart. Even now it stirred her desire... and her guilt. "Solomon Cotter doesn't belong here."

"I say he does, but instead of arguing," he raised an age-spotted hand, "we will let Revel decide when he gets here."

Talking with her father about Revel was worse than arguing over hiring workers. Her shoulders tightened. So much for coming outside to relax. "I'll ask Sam to stay here for a few weeks on a trial basis."

"Wait and ask Revel about it."

The hard bench irritated her back, so she stood. "Revel isn't coming home."

"Oh, yes he is. On Wednesday a trader brought the message from Good Springs. Revel and Connor are coming through Falls Creek on their way to Riverside next month. Got some training to do with a security team or something like that."

"You got a message from Revel on Wednesday? Why didn't you tell me about it then? That was two days ago. I deserve to know these things, Father. I am the inn's manager."

He patted her arm. "Calm down, Peach. I didn't get the message Wednesday. That's when a trader brought it. He gave it to Solo. I just found out from him when I was in the stables this morning."

Eva looked across the dry lawn toward the stable block. A watery sensation gurgled behind her confused heart. "Why would Solo keep Revel's message from us— from me—for two days? He knows our situation. He knows we need Revel to come home."

Frederick shrugged casually. "He probably forgot. Can't fault him for that."

No, she wouldn't fault Solo for forgetting, not in front of her father, but there was more to it than forgetfulness. The suspicion she'd felt toward Solo when he first arrived flooded back. Was he angling for a job? Is that what this was all about? Was his flirtation with her a part of his plan?

The man from Stonehill stepped out of the bunkhouse with his pack over his shoulders. He stomped toward the stable, his unshaven face scrunched in a scowl.

Eva shielded her eyes with her hand. "Where is Sam going?"

"Hm?" Frederick turned his upper body to look in that direction. "Who is Sam?"

Eva didn't answer as she watched the stable. A moment later, Sam emerged from the stable's archway, leading his saddled horse. That wasn't enough time to tack a horse. Solo must have saddled it for Sam while he was in the bunkhouse getting his pack.

From behind her Frederick said, "Looks like he's leaving."

"Not without an explanation." Eva raised her skirt and jogged toward the stables. "Sam? Sam, wait! Where are you going?"

He buckled his pack onto the back of the saddle. "Home."

"Now? I thought you were interested in the stable manager position."

"I was."

"What happened?"

He mounted his horse and turned the reins to maneuver the animal around her, but he never looked her in the eye. "You already have a stable manager. Ask him." He kicked his horse and rode off.

Zeke dashed out of the stable block, laughing as his puppy chased its tail. Solo walked out after him. He had the lead line draped over his broad shoulder and an easy grin for Zeke that instantly reached his eyes when he spotted Eva. He touched the brim of his hat to greet her, and Zeke did the same, imitating his new mentor.

Everything in her told her to march up to Solo and demand answers. Why did he hold back the message from Revel for two days? Why had he sent away a potential new employee? Why was he really here?

But Zeke bound over to her first. "Did you see me riding King, Mama?"

She smiled at her son and made sure her tone held the joy he deserved to hear rather than the anger she felt toward Solo. "I sure did, sweetie."

"Did I look big?"

"Yes, so big." She reached out to smooth his hair, and he flung his arms around her waist. Even though he'd been outside all day, playing and sweating and riding, he still smelled like her baby. She pulled him close for a rare mid-day hug and picked a bur out of his hair. "Did you tell Mr. Cotter thank you for letting you ride King?"

Zeke pulled away. "Thank you, Mr. Cotter."

Solo tousled Zeke's hair, which Eva had just smoothed. "You're welcome, partner." He looked at her then. "I told him he can call me Solo."

When she didn't reply, Solo's expression changed. Concern clouded his hazel eyes. He furrowed his brow as if asking her what was wrong.

She said nothing. He knew what he had done wrong. He'd held back Revel's message and sent Sam away without permission. Maybe with a look she could invoke conviction. Maybe he would confess to whatever game he was playing.

Instead, he turned his attention to Zeke. "We'll take King out again tomorrow. How does that sound?"

"Great!" Zeke shouted. He leaned down to his puppy and pulled on a stick the dog was chewing. "Did you hear that, Joshua? I get to ride King again tomorrow."

Solo hooked his thumbs in his belt loops and looked up at Eva with a satisfied grin, as if he was rightly taking his place in their lives, in her business, in her family.

She wasn't about to upset Zeke by confronting Solo right now, but she wouldn't leave Solo in his satisfied state for long. She leveled her gaze at him and whispered, "We need to talk."

A thick cloud passed above Solo as he stood in front of the stable block watching Eva's expression darken. It was more than the turn in weather that was chilling the air between them. She held her pretty chin higher than usual, and a thin ring of white outlined her dark irises. Whatever she needed to talk about had riled her feathers.

He squatted beside Zeke, who was playing tug-of-war with the dog. "Hey partner, why don't you take Joshua over to the big tree and tell your grandpa all about riding King."

Zeke obeyed him without question. He was the most well-behaved kid Solo had ever been around. Solo stood as Zeke happily ran to the other side of the yard.

When the boy was out of earshot, Solo stepped closer to Eva. He opened his mouth to ask her what was wrong, but she beat him to it.

"What do you think you're doing?" The force in her words matched the fire in her eyes. "You have a lot of nerve, Solomon Cotter!"

Well, it took a lot of nerve to stand close to this woman when she was mad. He almost stayed where he was to stake a claim in whatever battle she was starting, but he'd dealt with willful creatures his whole life. Gentleness built trust. He took a half step back and held up his hands. "Whoa, girl! You mind telling me what this is all about?"

"Don't *whoa girl* me."

"Take it easy."

"I'm not a horse."

"You're not yourself."

"You don't know me well enough to say that."

"I know you better than you think I do."

Something in her eyes reminded him of his mother— not how she usually behaved, just occasionally... once a month to be exact. Suddenly, it made sense to him. Not that women's troubles ever made sense to a man, but he remembered how his father handled his mother during her angry-for-no-reason moments. He slid his hands into his pockets and looked her in the eye. "Eva, I care about you. Take a deep breath and tell me what's wrong. Maybe I can help."

She slanted her head a degree and pursed her pink lips. "Your behavior. That is what's wrong. You had no right to do what you did."

Solo glanced around trying to understand the cause of her outburst. His gaze landed on the paddock. "Oh, that. I was teaching Zeke how to ride a horse. He was perfectly safe."

"He is not yours to teach."

His heartbeat picked up, heating his collar. "Maybe not, but your son is a good kid and eager to learn. He likes me. He follows me around asking questions all day, and I don't mind. You know why?"

Eva didn't answer, but a glaze of surprise briefly weakened her stubborn expression.

When she only stared, he continued. "Because I like him too."

She turned her face toward the bench where Frederick sat with her son. Zeke's arms gestured wildly as he demonstrated riding King. A faint grin curved Eva's mouth. Solo wanted to pull her close and kiss her. Maybe that would cure what ailed her. It would either cure her or ruin him. His respect for her outweighed his desire. "Look, I'm sorry I gave Zeke a riding lesson without asking you first. I know King is a big horse, but he's gentle."

She had every right to be concerned with her son. He couldn't imagine what she'd been through with losing a husband and raising a baby alone, but he was sure it made her worry about losing Zeke too. He'd seen the way she checked on her son all the time—out the windows during the day, peeking into their room every few minutes in the evening when Zeke was falling sleep. Maybe if she knew a man cared about her son too she would let go of some of the worry. He reached for her fingertips. "I will not let anything happen to Zeke, I promise."

She snatched her hand away. "That isn't what this is about."

His chest tightened. "Then what is?"

"I know what you are trying to do here."

"I'm trying to help you, that's all."

"Help?" She laughed one sarcastic note. "By trying to undermine my authority? By hiding messages from me and my father."

Her vague accusations hit him in the gut. "Wait, what?"

She propped both white-knuckled fists onto her hips. "You know what you did."

No matter how much he loved her lips, the words slithering from them were the same his mother always said when his brother had lied to get him in trouble. It always worked then, and the seething phrase still boiled his blood. He yanked off his hat to let the air cool his scalp. It didn't help. "I've worked my hide off for the past month for you and never once tried to undermine your authority. If you have a bone to pick, you'd better do it."

She forcefully stabbed the air with one thin finger as she spoke. "You held back Revel's message from us. Father said you got it from the trader two days ago but didn't mention it until today." She flicked her wrist at the road where a dust cloud still lingered from Sam's hasty departure. "And Sam told me you sent him away. You knew I wanted to hire him. I need Revel to come home and I need to hire another man. I trusted you and you betrayed me."

Her scathing allegations raked down his spine. Time of the month or not, no one had the right to talk to him like that. He wasn't the put-upon kid who took abuse anymore. He wasn't this woman's hired hand, too dependent on the work to stand up for himself. And he wasn't her husband, so he didn't have to suffer from her mood swings.

He had, however, promised her she could count on him and he wouldn't leave Falls Creek until she told him to. And he'd made that promise because he loved her.

Still did. He fanned his face with his hat then put it back on. "Eva, you're wrong."

"I'm not—"

He held up a palm to silence her and it worked. But before he could tell her why he'd told Sam to leave and that he didn't know what message from Revel she was talking about, she spun on her heel and stomped away.

Fine. He would let her cool off. She would probably go into the kitchen and gripe to Sybil. Maybe her sister would talk sense into her. He would burn up his frustration by working until dinner. Then he might be ready when Eva apologized to him.

CHAPTER TWENTY-FOUR

Breakfast aromas lingered in the dining hall while Eva listened to her father read from Ephesians. *"And be ye kind one to another, tenderhearted, forgiving one another, even as God for Christ's sake hath forgiven you."*

Rain pattered against the windowpanes as Frederick continued giving the short message he'd prepared for the inn's weekly Sunday morning service. Eva's gaze drifted to Solo, who was sitting at the next table. He looked smart in his pressed waistcoat and cravat. Her mind wanted to stay angry with him, but her soul recited the verse she'd just heard. *Tenderhearted, forgiving one another...*

She'd been anything but tenderhearted toward Solo during the past two days. Her stomach had burned since the moment she'd decided he must be trying to force his way into a job. The only thing that gnawed at her more than the tension between them was the conviction of knowing she needed to forgive him.

No matter what his plan was, it wouldn't work on her. Still, he had one last week at the inn. She needed to forgive him just as God had forgiven her.

A silent sigh flowed from her lungs, relaxing her stiff shoulders. Solo had done so much good for them. That should be her focus for the next seven days. Then, at the end of Solo's stay she would send him away with a sincere thank you for his work and food for the road, but no job offer and certainly not her heart.

She was the last person in the room to bow her head while her father said the closing prayer. It was the same prayer he prayed every Sunday. Zeke leaned against her side so she put an arm over her son. Her sister breathed softly sitting next to them. Surrounded by family, Eva still felt lonely. Of course she was lonely—she was a widow. Grief was to be her lifelong companion. She had reminded herself many times, but that didn't feel right anymore.

All that was left was a garbled hunk of confusion clogging her heart. Since Solo had been trying to maneuver her for his own gain, she could ignore the feelings for him that had been budding inside her. It didn't matter that he was courteous and gentle, loved her son, and had saved the harvest by working a month for nothing. And that he'd kissed her. The confusion he had caused in her was natural after all that, but now she could let it go.

Solo would soon be out of her life, but he had unlocked a door in her that she never thought would be opened. Now that it was, her feelings were more clouded than the autumn sky.

All that she had accepted about her lot in life—her widowhood and raising Zeke alone—came into question.

Did she miss Ezekiel or did she miss the ideal family she thought they would be?

Most days it was difficult to remember what her late husband looked like. She could conjure up memories of one aspect or another—grainy glimpses of his eyes or lips—but never all of his face at once. Even his image had departed her. What was she clinging to?

A wordless prayer lifted from her heart, a plea for God to give her peace if she was free to love again, and for Him to remove the guilt if she was no longer bound to Ezekiel.

Frederick said *Amen* and dismissed the family, guests, and traders, ending the service. As everyone rose from their seats, Sybil pulled Eva close and whispered, "Maybe the Lord has more for you in life."

Sybil's words sank in and left Eva wondering if it was God's answer to her prayer. Tears threatened to warm the corners of her eyes, but with a room full of people, she wasn't about to let them flow. She tucked a stray brown curl off Sybil's cheek and forced a smile. "Of course, He does. And for you too, Syb."

As the guests and Eva's family members mingled in the dining hall, Zeke tugged on her wrist. "I want to show you something, Mama."

"All right," she said as he led her out of the room. "Where is it? I don't want to go outside in the rain in my best dress."

"We're not." He led her past the staircase and into the reception room where he stopped her in front of the divan. "You sit here, Mama."

"Very well."

"I hope you like my surprise."

The preciousness of her child wanting to please her warmed her heart. "I'm sure I will."

Zeke hopped to the bookshelf and drew a single piece of paper out from between two books. After plopping down beside her on the cushion, he held the hand-printed page in front of them both. "Solo gave it to me."

As her son scooted close to her on the divan, she read the pristinely written top line aloud. "*The Moody Mare by Solomon Cotter.*" She glanced down the corridor toward the dining hall but couldn't see Solo. Looking back at the page, she lowered her voice. "Do you want me to read this story to you?"

"No, Mama. I'll read it to you. That is my surprise."

She scanned the first few lines. "Are you sure you know all these words?"

Zeke nodded and began reading the story to her. She tried to focus on the fable, but all she could hear was the sweet sound of her baby boy reading. When he reached the end, she wrapped him in a hug, wishing he would stay like this forever but knowing he was growing even now as she held him. She kissed the top of his head. "I am so proud of you."

He pulled away and looked up at her. "Then why are you crying?"

She dabbed a tear she didn't know had escaped her control. "Happy tears, that's all." She smoothed the thick fabric of her skirt. "Excellent job. Have you read it to Grandpa yet?"

"Not—" His gaze moved to someone behind her and he smiled. "Not yet."

She looked back to see Solo standing in the doorway. He had one hand in his trouser pocket and a humble grin creasing the lines around his mouth.

Zeke glanced between them. "You two probably need to talk." His young voice speaking mature words made Eva and Solo both chuckle.

Solo squeezed Zeke's shoulder as the boy passed him. "Thanks, partner."

Zeke grinned. "I think she liked your story."

"I'm glad to hear it." Solo stepped to the armchair across from the divan and sat opposite her. He propped his elbows on his knees and steepled his fingers. "Listen Eva, I—"

"No, don't." She stopped him not wanting to hear any more about his hiding the message from Revel or his chasing off her potential employee. "You and I have had a rough couple of days. I think it's best for everyone if we forget about everything."

"I can't."

"It's all right, Solo. I forgive you."

He drew his head back a degree and stared at her over the tips of his fingers. "You forgive me?"

"That's right. Even as God for Christ's sake has forgiven me."

He raised his scarred eyebrow. "Well, aren't you noble?"

"Sarcasm doesn't suit a children's writer, Solomon." She picked up the paper Zeke had left beside her on the cushion and scanned the sweet and moralistic tale. "You might have captured my son's heart, but I'm not so naive."

His jaw bulged while he tightened it. "You are crossing a line here."

"Me? How about you?" Her volume raised more than she intended, so she tried to calm down before anyone overheard them. "You tried to hide Revel's message from me."

He shot to his feet. "That is not true."

"And you got rid of Sam so I wouldn't hire him."

"You don't know what you're talking about."

Before she could counter him, he turned away and paced the rug in front of the bookcase, rubbing the back of his neck. After a moment he turned back around, his voice quieter but edged sharper than sewing sheers. "Why are you doing this, Eva?"

"I was trying to tell you I forgive—"

"The only way I wronged you was by making you feel something you didn't want to feel."

He was right about that. She'd spent a month feeling guilty and confused and infatuated. She watched the rain hitting the window so she wouldn't have to look him in the eye. "I will not fight with you anymore."

His boots softly thumped the floor as he walked to the divan and sat beside her. "All I want is to win your heart, but how can I? I can't fight a dead husband."

His words pierced her aching heart. How could he say such a thing? Whatever his game was, if she let it get to her, it was working. Teardrops hit her hands. She quickly wiped them away and whisked the others off her cheek. "I have a son to raise and an elderly father to take care of and an inn to run. I don't have time for this. The last thing I need is a man coming here, trying to take over my life."

"Eva, I'm not—"

She stood. "I'll honor the deal my father made with you, but the moment your forty days are up, you have to leave."

Pain darkened his eyes. "Are you sure that's what you want?"

She paused to take a steadying breath then managed a certain nod. "It's for the best."

"Don't do this."

"Solo—"

He reached for her hand but stopped before he touched her. "You need help with the farm until the new man starts. I can stay a few more weeks. Eva, don't make life harder for Frederick and Leonard."

His hand hovered in front of hers, waiting for her to reach out. Instead, she stepped back. "I'll manage. I always have. I don't need you, Solomon."

CHAPTER TWENTY-FIVE

Solo stepped over a manure pile on his way to the barn for the evening milking on his last day at the Inn at Falls Creek. Nothing had gone the way he'd planned. His stories remained unwritten. He'd worked harder for the past forty days than he had in the past year at the ranch. And Eva's heart was still as hard as a hoof.

As he walked into the open barn, the sound of milk spraying into a bucket came from the back of the dark building. Under the light of an oil lantern, Leonard was sitting on a milking stool beside the farm's crankiest cow. He turned his gray head away from the cow. "I can handle her tonight, son."

"What about the other three?"

"Already milked them."

Solo pointed at Leonard's bone-handled cane, which was propped against the barn wall. "Will you be all right after I'm gone?"

"I reckon." He glanced up at Solo as he slid a full bucket out from under the cow. "You finished the harvesting for me. Nothing but cows to tend to till the new man starts."

Leonard was making his job sound easier than it was. He slowly stood as if each vertebra of his spine needed a few seconds to mobilize. When he finally stabilized himself enough to reach for the bucket handle, Solo almost swooped in to lift it for him but stopped himself and waited to see if Leonard could indeed manage on his own.

Leonard grunted as he lifted the bucket and carried it out of the stall. He moved slower than he had before the stroke, but if he could do the work, Solo wouldn't step on his pride.

Even if his own was in tatters.

Nothing may have gone like he'd planned here, but he could leave Falls Creek with some satisfaction knowing Leonard survived his ordeal and the inn would have food for the winter. He leaned his shoulder against a rough post. "The gray leaf tea works wonders, doesn't it?"

"I'm not sure the medicine had anything to do with my recovery, not with the way my Claudia prayed for me. The doctor said I should be dead." He set the bucket down and wiped his palms together. "You still plan on leaving us tomorrow?"

Leaving us. The phrase scalded Solo's ears though it wasn't intended. He didn't want to leave the inn—to leave Eva—at all. He gave the door a quick check to make sure no one was outside, especially Zeke. "It's not by choice."

Leonard pressed his lips together in a grim line. "So you're giving up on her?"

"No. Not giving up. She told me to leave. Said she didn't need me."

"You believe her?"

"Not for a second, but I have to respect her decision."

Leonard chuckled sardonically. "Oh, she'll have her respect. She'll deny herself a husband and deny her son a father and send away the best man we've had on this property in decades, but she'll have her respect." His cheeks reddened as he scoffed. "That stubborn girl!"

Solo wished he hadn't said anything. He didn't want to upset the older man, especially on his last day here. "I'm sorry."

"Not your fault, boy." Leonard blew out a groan then stared at the dirt floor. "When do you leave?"

"Tomorrow. First light."

"Where you headed?"

"Back to the ranch in Riverside."

Leonard nodded. "Got a good job there?"

"Good enough." Just thinking about going to the ranch made his neck begin to ache. He rubbed it to no avail. "I only have to work one more year for the ranch to earn forty acres."

"Is that what you want? To have your own farm?"

"A horse farm, yes sir. It used to be." Solo looked out the open barn door at the darkening hills that rolled to the bleak southern horizon. "But it isn't all I want anymore."

Leonard gripped his cane's handle and leaned on it, the tone of his voice solemn but sure. "There are three truths that make life a lot simpler. Know what they are?"

Solo thought back to the frequent and fruitful lectures his granddad used to give him while teaching him how to train horses. "Let me think… We all will die, we all can be saved, and tomorrow is a new day."

The older man raised his silver brows. "All facts. But the three truths I'm talking about will change your life in this fallen world if you understand them."

He didn't try to guess again.

Leonard pointed one arthritic finger into the air. "There will always be something wrong with your circumstances." He raised a second finger, its knuckle more swollen than the first. "There will always be something missing from your life." Then a third finger. "There is nothing you can do to change either of the first two truths." He pointed his three raised fingers at Solo. "You accept those truths, and it'll cut your frustration in half."

Even half the frustration Solo felt with Eva was enough to ruin any man's mood. The same powerful spirit he loved about her was the very force that was keeping him away. She was impossible.

Leonard's advice was well-intended but irrelevant, not to mention depressing. Part of Solo wanted to lie down and die, and part of him wanted to break something. "Right, well, Eva doesn't want me here, so I'm leaving tomorrow."

Leonard shook his head. "Still don't understand, do you?"

"I guess not."

"When most men have trouble with a lady, they have to be told the answer is in giving the woman what she needs. Not you. You got that part, but you still don't know how to handle her." A faint grin deepened the creases around Leonard's mouth and he held up his three fingers once more. "There will always be something wrong, something missing—"

"And there is nothing I can do about it," Solo repeated the third of Leonard's so called three truths.

Maybe the stroke had done more than slow the older man's speech and stride. Of course Solo wanted to meet

Eva's needs. She needed him, his help, his affection. She was just too obstinate to see it.

There was truth in what Leonard was saying, but it didn't apply to Solo's relationship with Eva. Unless this was Leonard's way of telling him this situation was hopeless. Solo pushed away from the post he was leaning against. "My leaving is probably for the best then."

Leonard waved a hand as if shooing Solo away. "You'll understand one day, son."

CHAPTER TWENTY-SIX

Bailey walked along the dirt driveway beside Lydia as they left the house to go into the center of the village. She checked the tree-lined road in both directions out of habit—not that a car would zoom past and run them over. Clumps of manure dotted the road, attesting to the Land's favored mode of transportation.

Lydia held the two blue dresses the seamstress had made. Bailey opened a hand to her. "I can carry those if you want."

"Since Mrs. McIntosh hasn't met you yet, it would probably be best if your unusual alteration request came from me."

She hadn't meant to make things difficult for her hosts. "Did you already pay her to make my clothes?"

"Not directly." Lydia kept her gaze forward. Her chin lifted slightly as her voice filled with pride. "Since I'm the physician, my profession is village-supported."

"Meaning, you take care of them and they take care of you?"

The afternoon sun brightened Lydia's golden-brown eyes as she smiled a little. "That is one way of saying it."

The economy in the Land was still a mystery to Bailey. There was plenty to eat at the Colburn table, yet they didn't farm other than keeping a few chickens and one dairy cow. Someone from the village stopped by almost daily with a basket of vegetables or a sack of flour. Maybe John Colburn had an arrangement with the growers as Lydia did with the seamstress. "Is your dad's position also village-supported?"

"Yes, all the overseers in the Land are, as are our schoolteachers."

"What does everyone else do? Barter and trade?"

Lydia nodded. "Everyone works and everyone eats."

Bailey didn't want to be the exception. She'd helped with the hay harvest this week, but that was over now. Connor seemed to have the barn chores under control and still had time to study with John and train the security team. Lydia and her father shared the cooking, and everyone pitched in with housework. There didn't seem to be much Bailey could do to earn her keep. She dipped a hand into her empty jeans pocket and missed having cash. "I'll pay you back somehow."

Lydia tucked a windswept strand of hair behind her ear. "That won't be necessary. You are our guest."

Bailey had come to the Land to start a new life—one that didn't include handouts. "I can earn my own way. I could help with the vegetable garden."

Lydia's eyes widened. "You could?"

"Sure." At the thought of tending a garden, a bubble of joy rose to the top of Bailey's heart, and she didn't try to pop it. "I'd be happy to."

"Happy to," Lydia repeated quietly, as if the phrase were unfamiliar.

"Yeah, you know, I would really enjoy it."

Lydia shook her head and her loose bun wobbled. "No, I know what the phrase means. I just haven't heard you say you were happy before. I suppose that's reasonable considering the outside world's condition."

Bailey mindlessly followed Lydia onto the road, overcome by what she'd said. It was true this was the first time she'd felt a glimmer of happiness since first seeing the Land. "I hope I didn't seem ungrateful before."

"Well—"

"I wanted to come here. I was delighted when I learned I had family somewhere in the world, and I prayed I'd be able to make it here to meet all of you and live in this beautiful place. It's just that..." She watched the tall grass along either side of the road ripple as the breeze blew across it. It bent in waves reminding her of the ocean. "It's just that with everything that happened at the beach when we got here and losing Tim... it all sort of soured my arrival."

She didn't know what she expected Lydia to say, but she let silence float between them. The road's sandy gravel crackled under her hiking shoes. The thick foliage of the gray leaf trees rustled, and birds sang to each other in the limbs overhead. The lack of traffic and trains and unnatural noise made her want conversation.

After a long moment, Lydia said, "What happened that night soured your arrival for us too." A faint but sweet smile warmed Lydia's face. "But I'm glad you're here."

Bailey's heart lifted. The joy bubble grew. "You are?"

"Yes, and so are my father and Connor."

John had made her feel welcome from the beginning, but she had assumed most of that was his profession. He was the pastor of the village church. He had to be kind to strangers. And even though Connor's suspicion had cooled once they had found Tim's possessions and he'd finally believed Bailey's story, it was hard to imagine the Land's first outsider was glad another had made it here.

Still, Lydia wouldn't have said it if it weren't true. If they could be glad Bailey was here, she could be too. "Thanks. That makes me feel better."

"We don't expect anything from you, but since you seem to enjoy work, we can arrange it."

"I do. It's kind of essential for me."

"I understand. We will have to find you something other than gardening though. Sophia is preparing the vegetable garden for a late crop."

"Oh." Bailey tried to hide her disappointment by looking away.

The road turned from gravel to smooth cobblestones as it descended a short incline through a tunnel of trees. The thick foliage cast speckled shadows onto the picturesque road. She deeply inhaled the gray leaf trees' scent. It reminded her of why she wanted to come to the Land the first place. "Do you need help with the gray leaf?"

A horse-drawn buggy passed. Lydia greeted the man driving it. Her smile faded when she looked back at Bailey. "I already have an assistant."

"Right, Sophia. She's awesome. I meant I could help you with your gray leaf research. I'm a plant biologist. That's how Justin found out about me; he wanted someone to analyze the gray leaf tree saplings and saw my name on a list of professional researchers." She stopped herself from telling the whole story, wanting to focus on the present. "I could look over your research notes, if you like."

Lydia stopped walking, her eyes wide. "You could?"

"Sure. I'd love to."

"That would be wonderful! Sophia recently discovered a baffling phenomenon with the gray leaf vapor. I'd be most appreciative if you would lend your expertise." After a quick tuck of her loose strands of hair, Lydia smiled and started walking again, still hugging the dresses. "Oh, Bailey, you might be the answer to my prayers."

CHAPTER TWENTY-SEVEN

The sun was still asleep below the horizon, making Eva wish she could have stayed beneath her comfortable quilt. If she crawled back into bed and a hard enough sleep smothered her, she could skip this day completely and not have to watch Solo leave Falls Creek. But her son would soon wake up and need her care, and an inn full of guests would need her too.

Her hand slid along the dull wooden rail as she descended the stairs to the dark lower level of the inn. The light of a single lantern flowed from the kitchen, but Sybil wasn't in there. A large mixing bowl and several utensils waited on the counter for their ingredients, and the freshly stoked oven warmed the room. Eva scanned the countertop on the far side of the long room. Sybil's egg basket was gone.

Eva carefully closed the side door as not to make noise and wake anyone before dawn. Then she walked across the dew-covered lawn to the chicken coop where Sybil's lantern illuminated a fraction of the property, hovering like a firefly over the laying box.

"Sybil," Eva called to her sister as she approached so she wouldn't startle her.

Sybil craned her neck around the coop. "Eva? What's wrong?"

"Nothing. I got up a few minutes early and thought I'd see if you needed help."

Disbelief laced her sister's voice. "Help gathering eggs?"

"Sure. Why not?" She held the laying box's lid open while Sybil drew out the fresh eggs.

"You haven't come to the coop since I was little and Mother made gathering eggs my chore permanently."

Eva remembered their childhood chores well. "Yes, and I always wished she had given me the coop and given you the mopping."

A sly smile curved Sybil's mouth. "It's too late to trade chores now."

Sybil was quiet as she filled the egg basket. When she was done, she stepped back. Eva lowered the lid and removed Sybil's lantern from a hook on the side of the coop. As they walked away, Sybil asked, "Why are you really up so early?"

Eva wasn't able to think of an answer. A faint gray glow in the eastern sky made the stable block's silhouette visible. The slight ability to see everything made it seem like she couldn't see anything. Her feelings for Solo were just as murky. She tightened the shawl around her cold neck. "Solo's forty-night stay is over. He's leaving today."

Sybil slowly walked with her toward the inn. "I know. I packed him a sack of food for the road. He came into the kitchen after dinner last night to thank me for all the delicious meals over the past few weeks. He said my venison roast is the best in the Land." She took one hand off the basket handle and put it over her heart as if swearing. "His words, not mine."

"He is right about that."

"Thank you." Sybil's tone softened. "Are you up early to say goodbye to him?"

"Hardly."

"What then?"

Eva held the lantern out to light their path across the damp grass. "I'm preparing for a busy day, that's all."

"You are a terrible liar."

"You sound like Mother." She meant it as a joke, but Sybil went silent.

Eva stopped walking and faced her sister. "I'm sorry. It's just that… everything feels wrong. It's like I'm fighting against something I can't see or name."

Sybil's caring eyes narrowed. "Because of Solo?"

She could no longer hold back the truth—from her sister or herself. "I care about him… very much. At least I did. I felt something for him too. I know it's wrong but—"

"Why is it wrong?"

"Because of Ezekiel." As soon as the words came out of her mouth, she realized how illogical it probably sounded to a person who hadn't lost a spouse. "I know it doesn't make sense to anyone else, but it's how I feel."

Sybil tilted her chin. "You are allowed to love again, Eva."

She almost dismissed her sister's words, but they echoed deep in her soul. Sybil was right: she was free to love again. Their father had said as much too, and she hadn't listened to him. There was nothing biblically wrong with a widow marrying again, in fact, there were verses encouraging young widows to marry. She stared down at the lantern's warm flame. "You're right, but I have spent so many years convincing myself it would be wrong. Still, with Solo... there is more to the matter than allowing myself to love, especially with his behavior last week."

"His behavior?"

"Father told me a trader gave Solo a message for us from Revel, but Solo kept it back for a couple of days."

"What was the message?"

"Nothing new. Just that Revel and Connor are coming through Falls Creek on their way to Riverside soon. It was the same message he wrote us last month. Anyway, he—"

Sybil raised a finger. "Why would a trader give Revel's message to Solo instead of to you or Father?"

"I don't know. But when I found out, I marched right over to the stable block to ask Solo about it, and low and behold, he had just chased off a man I was thinking of hiring."

Sybil's skin lightened as the first hint of morning light crested the earth. "The traders usually give messages to you as soon as they arrive or once they settle in. They wouldn't give a message for the family to another guest."

"That's not the point."

"And if a trader *did* deliver a message to Solo, why wouldn't Solo tell you immediately?"

"Because he didn't want me to know Revel was coming through so I would hire him for the stable manager job."

Sybil's eyebrows drew into a tight crease. "But Father gave you authority to hire. No message from Revel would matter if you wanted to hire Solo."

"Right, but…" As Sybil's dissection of the situation sank in, Eva lost faith in her original judgement. "What are you getting at?"

Sybil glanced at the door then lowered her volume. "I doubt there was a message at all. Not a new one anyway, and not given to Solo. Father probably mixed up a few memories and… you believed him."

Eva recalled the confusion Solo claimed when she had confronted him at the stable block that day. She looked up at the window of the corner room where Solo would be sleeping. Regret made her stomach lurch. "If you are right, I behaved cruelly toward Solo."

Sybil cocked her head. "Is that why you told me the kiss you and Solo shared meant nothing and that you were looking forward to him leaving here? Because of Father's story?"

"That and him chasing off Sam."

"Sam?"

"From Woodland. I planned to ask him to stay and work as stable manager for a trial period, but Solo told him to leave."

"Surely, Solo had a good reason."

Eva had been so furious with him that afternoon, she didn't remember what his excuse had been or if he had offered any. "I don't remember what he said. I assumed he was angling for the job."

Sybil gently squeezed her forearm. "Oh Eva, you have to talk to him. Hear his side of the story."

Could she have believed one of her father's wrong memories and been so angry with Solo that she didn't give him a chance to defend himself? He had said his only wrong was in causing her to feel something she didn't want to feel. The more she thought about it, the more she realized he was right. How was everyone right about her life and her heart but her?

The eastern sky lightened. She raised the lantern to put out its flame. "I've been such a fool, Syb. So heartless. And after the way he helped us too…"

"Do you love him?"

Eva paused to ponder the feelings in her heart. If Solo had done nothing against her or against her family, she had no reason for any ill feelings toward him. With that murkiness skimmed from her heart, all that was left was admiration, gratitude, attraction… affection. "I believe I do." She stared up at the last star clinging to the sky. "But I need more time."

"Then tell him you're sorry and ask him to stay. He's a reasonable man; he will forgive you."

Her sister made it sound simple. "I will try. When he comes down for breakfast, I'll invite him into my office to talk."

Sybil smiled. "Close the door so you can have privacy. I'll keep Zeke busy if he gets curious."

"Syb, you truly are the best sister I could imagine."

"I would do anything to help you find love again."

As they walked into the house, Eva remembered the way Sybil had looked at Isaac Owens. She held the door open for her sister. "Maybe someday, I'll be able to return the favor."

Solo rubbed his tired eyes then waited for his vision to adjust to the dim light in his room so he could pack his satchel. Missing half a night's sleep stifled his usual early morning verve. At least he'd had the foresight to load the wagon last night. All that was left to do this morning was clear his room and hitch up the horses.

He emptied the desk drawer and slid his papers into the satchel, save for two trifolded pages. On the outside of one he wrote *Zeke* and on the other *Eva*. He folded the letters once more and slipped them into his shirt pocket. With a long breath he paused and imagined delivering those letters. His empty stomach churned.

One lonely star still shone above the trees outside his window. It would be brighter out by the time he hitched the wagon to the two horses—King and the horse he'd borrowed from the ranch in Riverside when he'd fetched the doctor for Leonard. The older man had shown tremendous strength in his recovery during the past few weeks and had been generous with advice when Solo said goodbye last night. His wise words didn't seem applicable, but Solo was still grateful.

All that mattered now was leaving here at peace with Eva so he would be welcome to stay the night at the inn whenever he passed through in the future.

If he passed through.

With only a year left to work at the ranch before he earned his own land, he might not travel anymore. That suited him just fine. Maybe he would ride to the mountains when he needed to get away from Riverside. If the aching abyss of his bachelorhood grew too painful, he could ride past the foothills into the supposedly deadly mountain terrain. Either he would have a grand adventure with whatever was out there or he would be put out of his misery by whatever had stopped past explorers.

He gave the room one last scan, both looking for any forgotten items and bidding farewell to the place that had been home for the past forty nights. Then he tugged on his boots, slung the satchel's strap over his shoulder, and closed the door quietly behind him.

The moody house was dark and quiet while the other guests still slept. Downstairs, a solitary lantern burned in the kitchen. Solo poked his head into the long, stark room to say goodbye to Sybil, but she wasn't at her usual post.

The door to Eva's office stood open. Such a shame she kept her door open but her heart closed. He drew the letter for Eva out of his shirt pocket and tucked the paper for Zeke into his back pocket. Stepping inside, he laid Eva's letter in the middle of her messy desk. She might not even read his letter once she realized it was from him. Or maybe she would read it and decide not to believe him when he poured out his heart to her. She was good at that. His fingers burned to pick the letter back up, but his feet knew better. He swiftly left the office and hiked to the barn.

Once the horses were hitched to the wagon, he led them out of the stable and checked the wheels as it rolled. He gave King a long pat. "It's time to go, old boy."

King lifted his head, half with pride, half wanting to have his neck scratched. Solo indulged him, then checked the lines. As he walked around the wagon, something across the yard caught his eye.

Zeke was dashing toward the stable block with his puppy running behind him. "Solo! Solo! Are you leaving before breakfast?"

Solo met him in front of the horses. "Yes, but not without saying goodbye to you, partner."

Zeke's round eyes searched him as if his mind was working to find its words. Finally, he blurted out, "I'll miss you so much!"

"I'll miss you too." He knelt to be eye-to-eye with the boy and drew the paper from his back pocket. "I wrote a special story just for you. Read it anytime you miss me."

Zeke accepted the paper with both hands, his small fingers seeming too delicate to belong to a boy who had helped him with farm work for the past forty days.

Solo tousled his hair. "You're a good kid, Zeke. Going to make a fine stable manager here someday." His nose burned as emotion welled in his throat. "Be good for your mama."

Zeke smiled. "If I am will you bring me another puppy next time you come?"

That got a chuckle out of him. Why did it always feel good to laugh when he was fighting back tears? He looked away. "Probably not a puppy, but I'll be mighty proud of you."

Zeke's smile dimmed slightly, the reality of their separation clear in his eyes. He wiped his nose with the back of his hand. "I'll be good, I promise."

Everything in Solo made him want to unhitch the horses and unpack the wagon and take Zeke by the hand and march into the house and demand Eva see how much he loved them and wanted to make a family with her. But he couldn't. He loved her too much to make demands. She had commanded his respect since the first time he met her, and she would have his respect as he left here today, even if his guts ached like he had been trampled in a stampede.

He stood and gave Zeke's shoulder a squeeze. "Tell your grandpa I said goodbye. I talked to him last night, but he might not remember much. Keep an eye on him for me."

"Yes, sir."

Solo pointed at the puppy. "And keep training Joshua. He'll be a good working dog."

Zeke's nose turned pink. He started to say something but stopped and threw his arms around Solo's waist, hugging him tightly. "I don't want you to leave."

"I know. I don't want to leave either." He rubbed Zeke's little back. "Sometimes we have to do hard things. This is one of those times, partner." He pulled the boy away and held him at arm's length. "We both have to be strong just like when you helped with the harvest. That was hard, wasn't it? And when you learned how to sharpen the thresher blades. That was hard too, wasn't it?"

Zeke nodded, tears making a jagged line down his freckled cheeks.

"Well, this is hard, but we are strong men, up for the challenge." His pep talk was more for himself than the boy. "Give King one last pat then wave to us as we pull away, all right?"

Again, the little boy nodded. He patted King while Solo climbed up to the wagon bench. Then he stepped back and crinkled his chin as he tried not to cry.

Solo released the brake and shook the lines to make the horses go. His insides ached more every second. He tipped his hat to Zeke then fixed his gaze on the distant horizon and drove the wagon away from Falls Creek.

Footsteps resounded from the guest rooms upstairs, so Eva dashed into her office to tidy up before Solo came down to breakfast. She stopped in front of the mirrored sconce by the bookcase and checked her reflection. Morning light broke through the windows, giving her skin a rosy glow. She pinched her cheeks anyway.

The heavy beat of boots thudded the staircase. She peeked down the hallway. It wasn't Solo. Her stomach flip-flopped inside her. He was usually the first guest downstairs in the mornings.

She turned to her desk to straighten the pile of inventory lists, but her heart dropped when she saw a folded piece of paper on top of the stack. Her name was written on the outside of the letter in Solo's neat handwriting. She opened the precisely folded note.

Dear Eva,

Since you don't want me to stay, I must leave you with the truth. I never received a message from any trader. If I had, I would not have kept it from you.

I caught Sam stealing tools from the barn. That is why I told him to leave Falls Creek immediately. Maybe I should have asked you first, but I didn't want him around long enough to steal anything else from you.

I don't want to leave here this morning, but I will because you told me to go. I care for you and Zeke more than I have ever cared for anyone. I pray God's very best for you.

All my love,
Solo

The ache in Eva's heart tightened with each sentence she read. Sybil had been right; Frederick had probably gotten confused when he told that story about the message from the trader. She should have trusted Solo, but she ruined it. He loved her and had protected her and her family. And now he was gone.

The barely sealed scars of her heart threatened to burst open. She dropped the note and rushed out of her office, ignoring a guest's cheerful greeting, and let the side door slap against the house. Her feet didn't stop until she passed the iron bench and fell to her knees in front of Ezekiel's gravestone, weeping like she did many times in the first few months after his death.

Tears blurred her vision as she stared at the polished stone marker. "Why did you have to leave me?" As soon as the habitual question passed between her lips, she realized today it was not meant for Ezekiel, but for Solo.

And she knew the answer.

Solo left because she had refused to hear the truth— from him and from her own heart. Now it was too late.

She lifted her face to the pale lavender sky. Her throat burned. "Lord, after I lost Ezekiel, You bound up my heart so I could raise Zeke. You gave me the strength to face each day. I never thought I would love again… that it would be wrong of me. Just when I allowed myself to admit I love Solo, I lost him too. And here I am, back at my husband's grave. I don't know what to do, or if there is anything I can do. Please help me."

She paused, hoping the Lord would answer.

No voice came.

She pressed both hands over her throbbing heart. "If I am meant to be alone, I can raise my son and run the inn and take care of my family but not while holding my wounds closed. I need you. In my weakness, You are strong."

Tears dripped onto her hands until the sun crested the earth, casting sidelong shadows over the dewy grass. Zeke called out from the side door. "Mama?"

She stood slowly, her skirt damp with dew. "I'll be there in a minute, sweetie."

He stayed on the stoop, his trousers too short and his hair a mess. "But I need you now."

Her son's simple plea sank into her heart, dulling the ache. He needed her, depended on her, just as she depended on the Lord. It wasn't the answer she was looking for, but it was the answer she needed.

In God's graciousness He had given her a child, someone who needed her love and attention. She had spent too much time focusing on what was missing rather than what was right in front of her. She wouldn't have had the blessing of Zeke without Ezekiel, but the Lord had also given her everything she needed to raise her son well.

Though her heart yearned for more and might always, she would live fully in the present with the people God had put in her life, foremost being her son. She gave the tombstone one last glance. "Goodbye, Ezekiel," she whispered and walked away from the grave.

CHAPTER TWENTY-EIGHT

An hour with the seamstress left Bailey more exhausted than a day of packing hay. She was looking forward to an evening alone in the quiet Colburn house. John was counseling a family in the village. Lydia and Connor had taken the baby with them to dinner at Levi and Mandy's house. And Revel was at the Fosters' farm where he'd spent the day working alongside his brother, James.

John had left a pot of stew simmering on the stove. It filled the kitchen with a warm, homey aroma that reminded Bailey of the Polk family. She lifted the pot's iron lid and inhaled. After ladling the stew into a bowl, she sat at the table—on the side by the hearth so her back wouldn't be to the door—and put her feet on the chair across from her.

Though the savory stew satisfied her taste buds, the lack of company reminded her of the lonely nights in her Norfolk apartment. Being by herself during the day never bothered her, but evenings had a way of underscoring emptiness. That was why she'd taken the job at the bar. Well, that and so she wouldn't starve.

As she dipped a heel of bread into the stew, her eyes followed the lines of the dark beams up the corners and across the ceiling. With no electronic appliances, the wide country kitchen held an old-world charm that made her feel like she had gone back in time. She'd wanted a quiet life, but this kind of silence was overwhelming.

After washing her bowl in the sink, she ambled around the room, imagining the seven generations of Colburns who had cooked and eaten and celebrated milestones here over the years, one large family after the next. Yet now it was stone quiet. A simple life must be enjoyable only if there were people to share it with. No wonder John Colburn kept his house full of guests.

She wandered into the living room—the parlor, they called it—to a bookcase with glass doors. The lettering on the books' leather-bound spines ranged from embossed gold to handwritten ink. She opened a glass door and perused several of the books.

There were classics she remembered from school—*The Scarlet Letter, Uncle Tom's Cabin, Shakespeare's Sonnets*—and many titles she didn't recognize. One book seemed particularly worn. *Between Two Moons* by Hannah Vestal. Probably a family favorite. Maybe she would enjoy it too.

As she reached for the book, the sound of the back door opening and then closing came from the kitchen. The whistling of a joyful tune flowed into the living room. She slid the book off the shelf and glanced at the wide doorway, waiting to see who it was.

Revel walked into the living room. When he spotted her, he did a double take and halted. "Oh, hello, Bailey."

"Hey."

"I didn't know anyone would be home this evening."

"Just me." She carried the book to the sofa and lowered herself onto its red velvet seat. "How did it go?"

A day's worth of sweat had darkened his hair. He smoothed it with his fingertips. "How did what go where?"

"Whatever you were doing today. How was your day?" She probably sounded desperate for conversation. She wasn't desperate—just glad to have someone around.

A slow grin reached his eyes. "Everything went well." He held up one finger. "I need a quick shower. I'll be right back." He jauntily hurried down the hall as if the prospect of talking to her excited him. At least he wasn't acting shell-shocked anymore.

Bailey opened the book and scanned the first page, not really reading it. The muffled sound of running water hummed from the downstairs bathroom. She thumbed through a few pages, but a book couldn't keep her interest when there was a person around.

A few moments later, Revel returned to the living room with wet hair and clean clothes. He hoisted his suspender straps over his shoulders and picked their conversation up where they had left off. "My day was fine. I helped James build a sheep pen." He plopped down across from her in the armchair where John usually relaxed in the evenings. A hint of mischief overtook his easy grin. "How was your afternoon with the dressmaker?"

Bailey chuckled, liking that he found her clothing struggle amusing. "I'm still wearing my jeans, aren't I?"

"Then you were victorious. Congratulations."

"Actually, Lydia and I reached a compromise."

He raised both eyebrows. "What did you have to concede to get trousers made?"

"Lydia said if I wear pants to church, it might be a distraction for the villagers. So, I agreed to keep the dresses for Sundays. I want to respect your tradition—"

"It's not *my* tradition," he interrupted. "I like your clothes."

"Your people's tradition then," she said, correcting herself and ignoring his compliment. "I'll wear the dresses to church on Sundays, and the seamstress will make clothes similar to mine for the rest of the week."

"A happy compromise."

"I'll get back to you on the happy part after I've worn a dress for a few hours on Sunday."

He laughed and the robust sound filled the cozy living room. She relaxed into the sofa's cushioned back. "Seriously though, I know Justin Mercer had a hard time with the culture here and caused problems. I'm trying not to come across like him because—for the most part—the way of life in the Land appeals to me. I'm grateful to be here."

"That will please John." He shifted in the chair but didn't take his gaze off her. "That's what you want, right?"

It wasn't about pleasing John or Lydia or anyone in particular, although she wanted their approval. It felt too complicated to explain, and she wasn't sure she had sorted it out herself. But the way Revel gave her his full attention made her want to talk more. "I'm trying to find a balance between being myself and being respectful. Things are very different here from what I'm used to."

He angled his head, still studying her. "Do you think you could be content living in the Land?"

First, Lydia had been surprised when Bailey expressed happiness, and now Revel was asking this.

Either she was giving off a negative vibe, or she'd kept too much to herself and left them imagining how they would feel if they were her. "Why do you ask?"

"I can usually get a sense of a person fairly quickly, but I can't figure you out."

So it was the latter then; she was a mystery. Her fingers traced around the letters on the cover of the book she held. Having been written in the Land, it contained a story no one in the rest of the world had read. There was much to explore here, which appealed to her as a scientist. "I believe I'll be content here one day."

He leaned forward and propped his elbows on his knees. His casual smile vanished. "If none of this had happened, what would you be doing with your life in America?"

"Trying to stay alive."

He didn't respond but only watched her, waiting for more.

"If everything had gone the way I wanted it to before the war, I would have moved out to the country. Planted a garden. Kept goats and chickens and—I don't know— befriended the locals, sold produce at the farmers market."

He lifted both hands as if she'd said something profound. "You pretty much described life here in the Land."

"You make this sound simple."

"It is." He chuckled. "Or at least it could be if you let it. You need to get out and meet people. Maybe travel around the Land."

"I was thinking the same thing." She set the book on a glass-topped side table beside the sofa and forgot about it.

"I wouldn't know where to start though. Have you traveled much?"

Faint dimples indented his cheeks as he grinned. "Yes. Some years I travel constantly, working with the traders. I never stay in one place too long. I've been to every village in the Land many times."

There was more to Revel than the suspenders-wearing hay loader she'd pegged him to be. He might be her best bet to finding her place in the Land. "Which village are you from?"

Once again, his grin flattened quickly. "I wasn't raised in a village. My family runs the Inn at Falls Creek."

Bailey's spine tingled with excitement. "There's an inn here? Where is Falls Creek?"

"About halfway between Woodland and Riverside."

"I have no idea where these places are."

He held up his left hand—fingers together, palm facing her—and traced it. "Imagine this is the Land. Most people live in the villages on the east coast which is about four hundred miles long." He dotted imaginary points along the outer edge of pinkie and palm. "Good Springs is a little north of center. Woodland is about forty miles southwest of here, and the inn is twenty miles southwest of Woodland near Falls Creek."

"What was it like growing up in an inn?"

He turned his face away and stared blankly across the room for a moment. When he looked back at her, his eyes held a sadness that made her sorry she'd asked.

"It's okay if you don't want to talk about it."

He shrugged one shoulder coolly, but it did little to lighten his expression. "Let's just say there is a reason I prefer to keep traveling… several reasons."

"I get it." She tried to veer the subject back to the location of his hometown rather than his feelings about it. "So, is Falls Creek near a village?"

"No, ma'am. It's out in the middle of the Land, beside a lonely, cold creek."

Yeah, no baggage there. She let it go for now. There was so much she needed to learn about this place, seeing as how it was her new home. She recalled the satellite image of the Land that Justin had shown her. "Justin said there are mountains that divide the Land. How far away are they?"

"About fifty miles inland from here. But we don't know if the mountains actually divide the Land."

"What do you mean?"

He lowered his volume even though no one else was in the house. "We don't know what is on the other side of the mountains or if there is another side. No one has ever gone into the mountains and come back to tell about it."

"How many people have tried?"

"I'm not sure."

"Anyone you know personally?"

He shook his head. "All the stories are old. Decades old, maybe. No one that I know of has gone to the mountains during my lifetime. Maybe not in my parents' lifetime either. But all the stories are the same. Whenever people go to the mountains, they never come back."

To Bailey it sounded more like superstition kept people from the mountains than any verifiable hazard. "What do you think happened to them?"

"Something bad."

"Like they got eaten by wild animals or taken captive by a savage tribe or what?"

He shrugged. "We don't know what is in those mountains. Could be a whole other civilization living over there. Or the Land might drop off into the ocean. We don't know."

That would explain the faded western half of the Land on the image Justin showed her. Whatever was there hadn't shown up on his satellite scan for the gray leaf tree molecules. The whole idea of the unknown fully piqued her interest. "How close to the mountains have you traveled?"

"Riverside is on the east bank of the river. There are a few farms on the west of Riverside. That's as close as I've been." He shuddered as if a chill had shaken his spine. "And that's as close as I hope I ever have to go."

CHAPTER TWENTY-NINE

Solo brushed King as he prepared to saddle him and ride out to the western pasture on his first day back on the ranch. Riverside hadn't changed in the forty days he was gone. Neither had the ranch. Or the stirring in his soul to do more with his life than raise horses to make another man prosper.

He swiped a curry comb over the horse with slow strokes out of exhaustion—not of body but of spirit. Everything within him yearned to return to Falls Creek, to Eva. If only he could have made her see the truth about him, made her acknowledge her feelings for him. He knew those feelings were there buried beneath her scars, even if she wouldn't admit it.

He shouldn't have left that letter on her desk yesterday morning. He should have confronted her. Yes, he'd needed to leave early for the ride to Riverside, but he shouldn't have let that matter. She wasn't a morning person; he could have used that weakness to his favor and gotten her to listen to reason. But he hadn't. He'd dropped a letter on her desk and left.

Left her, left the inn, left Zeke. Left the chance for the only life that had ever felt right.

He wished he still had his granddad for days like this. He tried to imagine what their conversation might be like if he told him he had found the woman he wanted to marry but she'd sent him away. King nudged him to keep brushing. It reminded him of how his granddad used to say the best conversations were with horses. After glancing around the dark stable, Solo moved closer to King's ears. "I miss her, old boy. Miss her something terrible. There isn't anything I can do. Even Leonard said so."

He thought about Leonard's inapplicable advice. "Instead of telling me to go after Eva, he said there would always be something wrong in life and there was nothing I could do about it."

King's ears turned.

"Oh, he said some other stuff too. Something about how I shouldn't give her what she wants." He eased up on the brush as he thought, and King leaned in for more strokes. "Maybe Leonard meant that I shouldn't care about what Eva said she wanted and I should have stayed at the inn. I sure wanted to, but it's too late now."

Hoofbeats approached the stable, snapping him from his one-sided conversation with King. His neck warmed as the foolishness of his behavior sank in. He was a grown man; he shouldn't talk out his problems with a horse.

"You in there Solomon?" his boss called from the doorway.

Solo swallowed his embarrassment, grateful his boss hadn't heard him talking to King. "Yes, sir."

"Well, get out here and take this worthless horse into the pasture." His boss cracked a whip at the horse Solo had ridden from the inn when he came to get the doctor. It was Frederick's horse.

Solo stomped toward his boss. "He isn't worthless. And he isn't yours to whip."

His boss narrowed his eyes. "I didn't ask your opinion. Now get him into the barn."

Solo took the horse's rope but didn't obey his boss. The horse didn't belong here, and neither did he. They both belonged at the inn. He squared his stiff shoulders. "I need to take this horse back to his owner at Falls Creek. I brought your horse back to you, so it's only fair. The Roberts family was grateful you let me swap horses that day."

His boss lifted his chin, a rare flash of concern easing his gaze. "Did the old man live?"

"Leonard recovered mostly. This is Frederick Roberts' horse. I should return him to the inn."

"Joe can take him when he goes through there on his way to Woodland next week."

The hope of returning to the inn quickened Solo's pulse. The excuse of taking the horse back wasn't working on his boss. Horses were often swapped between the inn and the ranches of the Land as travelers had needs. No one at the inn was missing the horse, but he was missing Eva. He took a step closer to his boss. "I have to go back to the inn, sir."

The man shook his head sternly. "You just came back from spending over a month away. If you want to claim your acreage next year, you'd better get to work."

Nine years down and only one to go, then he would be free and have his own land and could raise his own horses. But Eva's feelings might disappear by then. Urgency quaked his insides. He had to see her once more, to try again to win her heart. "Let me return the horse to the inn. Please. It's important to me."

"I don't care what it means to you. Do you think I'm running a charity here?" His boss spit on the ground and turned to walk away. "Get to work."

"I would only be gone a couple of days, three at most."

His boss rounded on his heel. "If you leave here again and it's not for work I've assigned you, you aren't coming back."

If he left, he would lose his job and the chance to own his own land. Without land he would always be at the mercy of others for work. But if he didn't go back to Eva now, he would always regret it. It wouldn't matter if he had all the land in the world if his soul was crushed. He straightened his spine. "I have to go."

"Then you're out of a job, Solomon. Don't come back here begging me for work."

Solo's blood pumped hard through his veins as he gave the decision one last moment of thought. Then with certainty he looked his boss in the eye. "Don't worry. I won't."

CHAPTER THIRTY

Eva followed along as Zeke read aloud from his storybook during their afternoon reading lesson. She turned the last page for him, and he snuggled close to her on the divan in the reception room. As he read the story's ending, she looked away from the book and out the window.

Tree limbs rustled across the road, swaying with the cold autumn wind that blew up from Antarctica. Before long, a layer of snow would blanket the road, and fewer travelers would visit the inn.

"The end." Zeke pulled away from her and closed the book. "Can we read one more story? From the book with the red cover?"

"Sure, sweetie."

While he hopped to the bookshelf pretending to be a bunny rabbit, the rumble of a wagon on the stone bridge drew Eva to the front window. She stood close to the glass to look to the east but couldn't see who was coming. Hoping it would be a trader with lantern oil, she hurried to the door. She glanced back at Zeke. "Start reading your next story. I'll be back in a moment."

"All right, Mama." Zeke flopped onto the divan and opened the thick story book.

The chilly air stung Eva's nose when she drew her first breath outside. She wrapped her shawl closer to her neck while the approaching wagon came into view.

A mismatched pair of horses—a brawny Shire stallion and a thin dun gelding—pulled the wagon to a stop in front of the inn. One man sat atop the wagon bench, but it was the only man she wanted to see. Her breath caught on a spike of excitement.

Solo climbed down from the wagon bench and patted King as he passed the stallion. He said something to the horse, but Eva couldn't hear his words.

The wind flipped the collar of his overcoat against his neck as he strode toward the inn. He locked his confident gaze on her but didn't smile. Maybe he was just passing through, or perhaps he'd left something behind and was only here to claim it and would leave again.

Everything within Eva wanted to dash down the porch steps, fling her arms around him, and beg him to stay. Somehow, she kept her feet firmly planted on the porch, wanting to hear why he had returned before she offered him the half of her heart that was still beating.

Solo stopped at the bottom of the porch steps and knocked the brim of his hat higher. He looked up at her, his voice flat. "Afternoon, Eva."

"Good afternoon, Solomon."

He pointed a thumb over his shoulder at the wagon but left his gaze on her. "I'm returning your father's horse."

Old habits told her to keep her chin raised and her tone curt, but she wanted to melt down the stairs into a sniveling puddle and plead for his forgiveness. She no longer needed her former hard facade, nor would she crumble. "I read the letter you left on my desk."

He said nothing. His eyes studied her acutely.

She walked to the edge of the steps. "I'm sorry for how I treated you. I misjudged you."

She waited for him to accept her apology, to say something, but he quietly watched her. Maybe after the way she'd behaved, it would be fair if he made her squirm. If the tables were turned, she might be tempted to do the same. No. The Solomon she knew was more mature than that.

Slowly, his expression softened as he chose his words. His low voice stayed steady and full, like it had been the evening they sat on the porch swing together. "*Forgiving one another, even as God for Christ's sake hath forgiven you.*" He climbed the first step as he quoted the verse from Ephesians. "Would you spare a bed for the night? I can trade two tins of lantern oil for a night in the bunkhouse."

She descended the top step, unsure of how she could keep her feelings to herself with him on the property for a night. "If that is what you wish."

A faint smile curved his lips. "Is that what you wish?"

No, it wasn't. She wanted so much more but wouldn't say it. There was one thing she could offer without giving herself away. "We need a stable manager. Father was right when he said you are the best man for the job. Would you consider filling the position… permanently?"

His smile flared then vanished and his gaze intensified. "I will consider it, but I didn't come here for a job, Eva."

His change in demeanor reminded her of the Sunday they had fought in the reception room, her dodging the truth of her feelings, him offended by her accusations. If her apology now hadn't ended their argument, she had nothing left to say. She blew out an exhausted breath and its white cloud was carried away by the cold wind. "Solo, I'm tired of fighting."

He pulled off his leather gloves. "I'm not fighting anything but my own desire. I think that might be true for you too."

"What are you saying?"

He slid his gloves into his coat pocket and climbed one more step. "I quit my job in Riverside. I don't belong there. I can go up to my cousin's horse farm in Good Springs and work. Mark would be glad to have me, but I doubt I would feel like I belonged there either. If you need me here, that's reason enough for me to stay. I belong here." He took another step and stood eye-to-eye with her. "But I want more than a job. I love you, Eva, and I want to spend my life with you. I want to make a family with you and Zeke."

She opened her mouth to speak but stopped when he took her hand in his.

"I know I'm not the first to love you, and I promise to never diminish what you had with Ezekiel." He glanced toward the barn. "A wise man recently told me there will always be something missing in life, something wrong in our circumstances, and there isn't anything I can do to change it. That's life in this fallen world. But I can promise to love you and Zeke with everything in me."

He climbed the last step and stood on equal footing with her on the top stair. "And just like a wild mare, I know you will need time to get used to me, so I'll take it slow. I'm not going anywhere unless you tell me to leave."

Sybil had been right: God had more for her in life, more than she could have asked or imagined. As Solo's words sank into her soul, she wrapped his callused hand with both of hers. "Stay. I want you to stay."

A satisfied grin warmed his eyes. He drew her close and lifted her chin with a soft touch. His gaze moved down her face as he lowered his lips to hers, not with the curious testing of the first kiss they had shared in the office that day but with the eager passion of a man declaring his love.

Before she could fully surrender to his kiss, he pulled back and took both of her hands in his. His breath was raspy as he spoke, his mouth still inches from hers. "I'll talk with your father, let him know my intentions."

She looked down at their joined hands, the heat between them taking all chill from the air. The Lord had carried her through tragedy and was now leading her into something she never thought possible. She lifted a silent prayer of thanks to God and decided to begin this new relationship with complete forthrightness. "Before you speak with my father…"

"Yes?"

"Since he isn't always in his right mind, I need you to make one more promise."

"Anything."

"No matter what words come out of his mouth now or in the future, I know this is what he wants for me. He told me as much when he was having a moment of clarity. So if he refuses you now or someday tells you to leave, promise me you will stay."

His quick response came with an assuring gaze. "I promise." He pressed his lips to hers, kissing her slowly, sweetly.

"No matter what comes, we will face it together."

"Together," she repeated on a hopeful breath. Her heart swelled inside her chest, what was dead now coming to life. The fullness of its beat flooded her with joy.

Long after dinner, the aroma of Sybil's delicious vegetable stew clung to the air in the dining room. Solo had pushed two tables together to make one long table so the whole family could eat together then play cards. Eva refilled the water cups before she sat beside Solo. He put his arm over her chair, so she leaned against his side.

Zeke smiled at them then reached down to pet Joshua. Her sweet son hadn't stopped smiling since Solo came back. He'd already asked her if one day soon Solo could be his daddy.

The burning gray leaf log in the fireplace warmed the room and offered its soft glow to the faces of those at the table. Eva studied each of them while her father shuffled the cards. Not everyone she loved was present; there would always be something missing, but never had she felt so content.

As Frederick dealt the cards, Zeke sat on his knees in the chair and his little dog curled up beneath it. Leonard winked at Claudia as he picked up the cards he was dealt and readied his hand. Sybil shifted in her seat beside Eva as if struggling to keep herself awake after a long day of work.

Footsteps thumped the steps as a trader from Northcrest descended the stairs. He turned at the newel post and walked into the dining room where he caught

Eva's eye. "Excuse me, ma'am. Sorry to interrupt your game. I forgot to deliver this message to you earlier."

Eva accepted the folded piece of paper. "Thank you." She hoped it was from Revel but didn't recognize the writing. As soon as she read the message, she looked at Leonard. "It is from Isaac Owens. His current employer found a replacement for him, so he can move here and start managing our farm immediately."

Leonard nodded once. "Excellent news!"

Claudia rubbed Leonard's back. "Praise the Lord!"

Frederick contracted his brow. "Who is doing what?"

As Solo patiently explained to Frederick what was happening, Eva glanced at Sybil, who perked up instantly. Her wide eyes were lit with an uncensored smile.

Eva leaned toward her and whispered, "You were right about God having more for me. Perhaps He has more for you too."

Sybil giggled and covered her grinning mouth with her fingertips.

Eva picked up her cards but instead of looking at the hand she'd been dealt, she watched her family. There would be moments of joy and laughter, such as now, and moments of tears and mourning, but so long as she remembered what God had done for her in the past, she could face the future with hope, knowing He would faithfully carry her through all things.

EPILOGUE

Bailey sat in the Colburns' living room, talking with Revel until the others came home. Connor and Lydia arrived first with little Andrew asleep in Lydia's arms. While she took the baby upstairs, Connor stayed in the living room, hovering as if he wanted to say something to Revel but couldn't in front of Bailey.

John arrived a few minutes later and the sound of running water came from the kitchen. Revel popped up out of John's chair as if he would be in trouble if caught sitting in it. Connor gave him an amused expression, and then they both looked at Bailey.

She didn't know why and didn't want to. "Okay," she said, drawing out the word. Picking up the novel from the side table, she backed away from the sofa. "Night, guys."

Revel flashed a warm grin. "Goodnight, Bailey."

"Night, Jeans," Connor said. Then he started telling Revel about an idea he was working on for starting a communications system between the villages.

Before Bailey turned into the hallway, John stepped into the living room and interrupted the guys' conversation. "Excuse me, gentlemen." The patriarch looked at Revel while holding up a folded piece of paper. "I received a letter from your sister, Eva, today. Have a seat, son. We need to talk."

As Bailey closed her bedroom door, the men spoke quietly in the living room. She wanted to keep the door cracked and listen to what they were saying but knew better. Whatever it was, John didn't sound happy about it. She was half intrigued, half concerned for Revel.

The twinge of interest growing inside her for these people made her feel alive. Having others around refreshed her with a sense of comfort and community. Whatever her life in the Land held, she hoped it would be in an active house surrounded by caring people.

She placed the book on the bedside table and ambled to the window. Darkness smothered the Land, but she wasn't tired yet. She peeled back the lacy curtain and stared toward the coast even though she couldn't see beyond the yard.

She wished Tim were here and could get to know John and everyone. There was no sense in thinking about how much she missed him. He had died giving her a chance at a new life. Still, she wanted to show him how that new life was taking shape. She wanted to tell him about sparring with Connor and going with Lydia to the seamstress and talking with Revel. She wanted to tell him that even though John Colburn was a distant relative, she felt a connection to him. She wanted to tell him maybe he was right when he said she could make a family out of friends.

Her mind told her not to, but her hands opened the wardrobe and felt around in the deflated backpack for the two-way radio. It was a step backward instead of forward. Maybe that was how she would eventually move on. She turned the radio on and glanced at the closed bedroom door as she increased the volume.

A man's scratchy voice was mid-sentence. "...out there please answer."

Bailey's heart thudded in her chest. "Hello?"

"Bailey? Bailey, is that you?"

"Tim?"

"Bailey, I can't believe it! You finally picked up. Are you really there?"

His hoarse voice sounded weak, more like the man he'd been after his family died during the water poisoning back in Virginia than the man she'd left on the yacht the night they found the Land. "I'm here, Tim."

"I've been trying to reach you for weeks."

"I'm so sorry. We thought you were dead."

"I thought I was too... a couple of times."

"Where are you?"

"I don't know where exactly."

"We looked everywhere along the coast. Have you tried to find the village?"

"I'm not on the same beach where you and the boys went ashore. I heard the gunfire and stayed in the tender for several hours. The ocean flipped me every which way, but I managed to hold onto the boat. The currents took me south and then into an estuary."

"Are you okay?"

"I found a survival kit in the boat's compartment. I have matches, a water filter, fishing gear—stuff like that. I don't have any insulin left. I'm not doing well, Bailey."

"Wherever you are, I will find you. The people here will form a search party with me." She paced the floor as she tried not to picture Tim sick and alone. "Are there any landmarks we can use to find you?"

"I followed the river inland a ways. Now, I'm camping on the shore. Landmarks?" He paused for a moment as if looking around. "It's dark right now, but all I've seen from here is mountains."

Bailey swallowed hard. "You're near the mountains?"

"Yes. Is that bad?"

"Don't worry, Tim," she quickly replied, hoping he wouldn't sense her fear over the air waves. "We will find you."

Thank you for reading my book. I'm so glad you went on this journey with me. More Uncharted stories await you! Are you ready for the adventure?

I know it's important for you to enjoy these wholesome, inspirational stories in your favorite format, so I've made sure all of my books are available in ebook, paperback, and large print versions.

Below is a quick description of each story so that you can determine which books to order next...

The Uncharted Series
A hidden land settled by peaceful people ~ The first outsider in 160 years

The Land Uncharted (#1)
Lydia's secluded society is at risk when an injured fighter pilot's parachute carries him to her hidden land.

Uncharted Redemption (#2)
When vivacious Mandy is forced to depend on strong, silent Levi, she must learn to accept tender love from the one man who truly knows her.

Uncharted Inheritance (#3)
Bethany and Everett belong together, but when a mysterious man arrives in the Land, everything changes.

Christmas with the Colburns (#4)
When Lydia faces a gloomy holiday in the Colburn house, an unexpected gift brightens her favorite season.

Uncharted Hope (#5)
While Sophia and Nicholas wrestle with love and faith, a stunning discovery outside the Land changes everything.

Uncharted Journey (#6)
When horse trainer Solo moves to Falls Creek, widow Eva gets a second chance at love. Meanwhile, Bailey's quest to reach the Land costs her everything.

Uncharted Destiny (#7)
The Uncharted story continues when Bailey and Revel face an impossible rescue mission in the Land's treacherous mountains.

Uncharted Promises (#8)
When Sybil and Isaac get snowed in, it takes more than warm meals and cozy fireplaces to help them find love at the Inn at Falls Creek.

Uncharted Freedom (#9)
When Naomi takes the housekeeping job at The Inn at Falls Creek to hide from one past, another finds her.

Uncharted Courage (#10)
With the survival of the Land at stake and their hearts on the line, Bailey and Revel must find the courage to love.

Uncharted Christmas (#11)
While Lydia juggles her medical practice and her family obligations this Christmas, she is torn between the home life she craves and the career that defines her.

Uncharted Grace (#12)
Caroline and Jedidiah must overcome their shattered pasts and buried secrets to find love in the village of Good Springs.

The Uncharted Beginnings Series
Embark on an unforgettable 1860s journey with the Founders as they discover the Land.

Aboard Providence (#1)
When Marian and Jonah's ship gets marooned on a mysterious uncharted island, they must build a settlement to survive. Love and adventure await!

Above Rubies (#2)
When schoolteacher Olivia needs the settlement elders' approval, she must hide her dyslexia from everyone, even charming carpenter Gabe.

All Things Beautiful (#3)
Henry is the last person Hannah wants reading her story… and the first person to awaken her heart.

Find out more on my website keelybrookekeith.com or feel free to email me at keely@keelykeith.com where I answer every message personally.

See you in the Land!
Keely

ACKNOWLEDGEMENTS

My sincere thanks to…

Marty Keith for recording encouraging videos on my phone so I would have pep talks at the ready, and for reading every one of my stories no matter how busy you are making your music.

Julie Gwinn for helping me brainstorm what was next and for encouraging me to continue with the Uncharted story.

Christina Yother for chatting with me whenever I needed to get my bearings, for being a faithful critique partner through this whole series, and for lending your farmhouse photo for the cover.

Rachel Keith for helping me give Zeke the perfect puppy, and for all that help with the horses.

Pam Heckman for reading early drafts that no one but a mother could love.

Rod Heckman for always finding the flaw in the slaw.

Megan Easley-Walsh for lending her gifts as the manuscript whisperer.

Annalise Hulsey for enthusiastically giving feedback on, well, everything. You were the first person to mark-up a draft of my writing, and I still wonder what you will think of every story I write.

To the expert voices who generously answered my questions on what to do with this series: Victorine Lieske, Carrie Schmidt, Ane Mulligan, Brenda Anderson, and Heather Gilbert.

ABOUT THE AUTHOR

Keely Brooke Keith writes inspirational frontier-style fiction with a slight Sci-Fi twist, including *The Land Uncharted* (Shelf Unbound Notable Romance 2015) and *Aboard Providence* (2017 INSPY Awards Longlist).

Born in St. Joseph, Missouri, Keely was a tree-climbing, baseball-loving 80s kid. She grew up in a family who moved often, which fueled her dreams of faraway lands. When she isn't writing, Keely enjoys teaching home school lessons and playing bass guitar. Keely, her husband, and their daughter live on a hilltop south of Nashville, Tennessee.

For more information or to connect with Keely, visit her website www.keelybrookekeith.com.

Made in the USA
Middletown, DE
16 October 2023